All About *Jane*

Judy MacDonald is such a flawless mimic of teenaged voices that this novel feels channelled . . . the whole book evokes that sense of the creepiness and waste of urban life usually found in genius pop music.
> *Quill & Quire*

The writer has nailed this character, never slipping out of her chosen narrative position, never inserting an image or a reference alien to her narrator's head or life experience.
> *January Magazine*

. . . part fantasy, part reality, part arty thriller, MacDonald gives us a brutal, erotic look at power, sex, submission and longing.
> *Vancouver Sun*

. . . Judy MacDonald's brave, brazen and consummately crafted novelistic debut . . . possesses a narrative sleekness that slithers under your skin and makes it crawl.
> *Toronto Star*

. . . This is uncommonly risky stuff, stirring up commonly buried truths. MacDonald makes us travel a quicksand territory between benign fantasy and criminal action; her probing of the relativity of innocence is both shocking and heartbreaking.
> *The Globe and Mail*

The fact that this is her debut novel is downright unnerving.
> *Scene Magazine*

grey

STORIES FOR GROWN-UPS
BY: JUDY MACDONALD

ARSENAL PULP PRESS
Vancouver

GREY
Copyright © 2001 by Judy MacDonald

ARSENAL PULP PRESS
103-1014 HOMER STREET
VANCOUVER, B.C.
CANADA V6B 2W9
arsenalpulp.com

The publisher gratefully acknowledges the support of the Canada Council for the Arts and the British Columbia Arts Council for its publishing program, and the Government of Canada through the Book Publishing Industry Development Program for its publishing activities.

Everything is made up. Some stories are more made up than others. Some of the made-up stuff is how I do indeed recall my life, or is where my mind has drifted to, and what I wrote down when I got back.

Some stories bear a weird relation to actual events. However, all of the characters in *Grey* (except perhaps myself) are fictional. At least in these pages.

The dedication includes lines from "Just in Time," by Betty Comden and Adolph Green (lyrics) and Jule Styne (music) (1956).

Text and cover design by Solo
Cover and interior illustrations by Amy Lockhart
Printed and bound in Canada

CANADIAN CATALOGUING IN PUBLICATION DATA:
    MacDonald, Judy, 1964-
    Grey

    ISBN 1-55152-109-1

    I. Title.
    PS8575.D645G73 2001   C813'.54   C2001-911424-9
    PR9199.3.M3114G73 2001

to Mark Connery

For love came just in time
You found me just in time
And saved my lonely life
That lovely day

Rolling Blue Concrete

I remember rolling concrete on a hot day. In some places it was painted blue and was full of yellow water. Peanut shells and bread floated on the surface. I could see no corners made from concrete. The water and the blue were behind fences. I saw the blue chipped in many places. I saw sad little monkeys hectored by people, and seals slick with that water.

I was excited. I loved this place, the animals. The concrete just rolled and rolled, tucked under every living thing. I dawdled too much, I guess. I was alone and in love by the time I got to the fence. My arms went out. I called, "Jerome, Jerome, Jerome."

The animal came to me.

"Jerome," I said.

When my family turned to find me, my arms were around its great long neck. The fence didn't really come between us.

"Jerome," I was saying, "Jerome."

The animal licked my face with a rough tongue, like a cat's but bigger. I was never happier. My family thought it was funny, but then they started to worry. This animal could bite. They saw its teeth, its lips. They came to me. I think a brother scratched the animal's muzzle. I looked over to my mother and smiled.

"Jerome," I said.

She must have smiled back. "Time to leave Jerome," she said.

I gave the animal one last strong hug. "He eats trees but kisses me," I said.

I floated back past the monkeys and seals. There seemed to be ice-cream cones stuck to the concrete everywhere – hard pink on grey. And children crying. But I floated, and the day floated, and I can still feel the dry heat and coarse tongue.

I held my mother's hand. My father's hand cupped the crown of my head. My brothers ran up to the monkeys, hollering and jumping up and down.

We came to the car. Dad let himself in, then reached over to all the other car-door buttons. Mom got in once we'd all safely closed the doors behind us.

In the Car, At the Computer

Bubba means breast. Bubba means milk. Bubba means a good thing. A sense of place. Love. He says, "I want bubba," and she gives it to him. He knows his name. He plays games. He is learning that he is alone, but not alone. He gets angry sometimes, because it feels bad, losing the sense of being everything. But he can almost always have bubba, which makes up for a lot.

"Me Leon," he says. "You momma. You Karen."

"You drive the car," he says. "Stop the car. I have bubba."

She's been caught doing it in the wrong places. It could be in the house, on the street, at a restaurant, when they go into the woods. When they visit. Karen sees the looks that some people give her. She doesn't know what the big deal is. Her own mother once said, "Some people might get the wrong idea."

Karen answered, "What, that I have breasts? It's actually true, you know. I do."

"But what about Leon?"

"Oh, he knows I have breasts for sure. Always has known, from a very young age."

"You know what I mean, Karen. Now he will *remember*. It's going to affect him."

You read book, I have bubba.
You sit on toilet, I have bubba.

I have bubba, cuddle truck.
I be naked.
I wear my shoes.
I keep my clothes on.

You lie on grass.
You eat your dinner, I have bubba.
You sew, I have bubba.
You stand up –

I open it myself.
I close it myself.
I want to go next door and have bubba.

Bubba while you walk.
Bubba while you sit in sun.
Bubba at the swimming pool.

Sometimes, Karen thinks what Leon comes up with is very funny. Sometimes it can be upsetting. But what really shocks her is the reaction of some grown-ups who hear one of his requests or see him suck. They tell Karen they are worried about what it's doing to her son, getting mother's milk at this late date.

She's heard kids his age talk about getting their soldiers to kill and police officers to kill while they push around little action figures. Kids even talk about astronauts killing. But that's okay. That's normal. "I hate you, I hate you. I'm going to kill you." To be expected.

Of course, Leon says these things, too.

There isn't any milk anymore; there is the memory of milk. Unless she trusts them, Karen doesn't tell people this. Leon got milk for three years, but then a couple of months ago he was lazy and she dried up. It didn't seem to bother him. He still likes the feel of her in his mouth.

She knows women who tried to breastfeed their first child without any luck. But they didn't always know it wasn't working. It can go on for days and even weeks, until someone who has experience notices the child's condition. People think breastfeeding is this simple natural thing that women just magically know about when the time comes. They're wrong.

He says, "You be naked, keep your underwear on. I have bubba."

She says, "Do I have to keep it on?"

Leon points his finger near her face and waves it around. He says, "I don't want to see. I not see your 'gina. I have bubba."

He says, "I will never touch a 'gina. Never!"

He sees his older sisters run around naked. He sees his mother's breasts. He knows he doesn't match. Still somehow, somehow, what she's got down there is best left hidden. Is dangerous and maybe dirty. This is an old and deep fear she shares with her son. It's upsetting to have it brought up again this way, but she doesn't push him about it.

He says, "You work on the computer, I have bubba." The floor lamp is on. Still, the room is dark at night. Light from the monitor washes over them. Leon's eyes are half-closed. His cheeks flush with a peace he will soon forget.

Writer's Block

It's near the end of July. Darcy is smoking again. A cigar, which was chic some years before, but isn't so much now. It's Darcy smoking it, though, and that gives the cigar a little something.

Darcy isn't quite seven yet.

She is in a bad mood, and has been for a few weeks. She hasn't talked to her mom and dad – or even her little brother, Joe – for a few days. That's because she took two of those stupid wooden mandarin orange crates, packed them with some clothes, filled a Barbie travel case, piled it all on the wagon her mom used for gardening at the rented cottage, and took off.

Darcy hitched north till she found a town she liked all right, then got a place on the outskirts of it. The town was small enough that this still meant she was in walking distance from everything, on her stubby grade-one legs.

She brought plenty of pencils with her, but no pens. She took a couple good erasers and a sharpener. Darcy can spell, and there is nothing an eraser can't fix anyway. The computer wasn't at the cottage to take, but it wouldn't have fit in the wagon anyway, especially with the printer, joystick, and other stuff it needed. Also, most of the games and stuff her parents bought for the computer were too babyish, boyish, or boring.

She's in her living room now, printing the words for a letter to her family. Printing them slow and deliberate.

Sory I run away.

Doan werry.

Feed me fish.

Joe doen tuch me stuff, ok

    Love

    Darcy

There had been a fight after her mom asked Darcy if she was excited about going back to school. For Darcy, it felt like the start of grade two was very far away, but also right up against her. Like a monster under the bed, never seen but always there, waiting.

"What are you looking forward to most?" her mom asked.

"Seeing my friends again, I guess."

"Yeah, and you'll be learning all sorts of new things, too."

"No I won't," said Darcy.

"Yes you will, honey. They'll teach you more math, and you'll read bigger books. Out loud, too, and –"

"What if I can't?"

"Darcy, don't be silly. You're a bright girl. It'll be fun."

"What if I can't? Like, I already learned how to print and I'm learning spelling –"

"The teacher said you were good with your lettering. You're careful."

"But mom, I worked hard. And, and. . . ." she was crying.

"Oh, honey," said Darcy's mom. She put one hand on her daughter's head and pulled the girl closer with her other arm. "There there, now. It's okay."

"So I can write the words in spelling. I mean, I can print. But now I'll have to write in writing but I learned the letters already – why do I have to learn them all over again?"

"Well, Darcy, it's –"

"What if I can't? What if all I ever know is printing? What if I fail grade two because of it? It's not fair. I can't. . . . Why did they. . . . I tried so hard with my letters, and now they'll all look different, and they're all hooked up together, and what if I can't figure it out? Why should I have to? I know my words."

Darcy was having a fit. It was no good trying to reason with her. But it broke her mom's heart to see Darcy like this. She felt she had to do something. She pulled her daughter even closer. She said, "There, there," and, "You'll do okay. You're a good girl, honey."

Darcy knew she was a good girl. She didn't know what this had to do with writing. She thought about being a teenager, trying to fit into a grade-two chair, sitting behind a grade-two desk, having classmates tease her while they trip over her big feet that poke out from underneath everything.

She stopped crying, and her mom – who was thinking about what to make for supper – decided that things had worked themselves out. Darcy, meanwhile, moved on to thoughts about what to pack. No room for dolls.

Back in the four-room cabin she is renting for herself, Darcy doesn't blame her mom, dad, or even her little brother, Joe, for what happened. She just couldn't take the pressure. She just needed a break.

After she finishes her letter to the family, Darcy puts it in an envelope, which she carefully addresses. Because she has no stamps, Darcy gets ready to go to the convenience store. It's not a very nice day. She still has trouble with laces, so Darcy puts on her rubber boots, which look sort of like turtles. She also wears her cute yellow raincoat with the duck-headed hood.

Orchard Mines prides itself for caring. The townsfolk notice strangers, particularly young ones who seem to be all alone. A lot of the people here are talking about Darcy. Some of them worry about the smells that roll off her from time to time when she comes around – cigars, maybe even whiskey. Others pooh-pooh the concern: "Well, maybe her daddy enjoys life," they say.

"So what's with this daddy?" say the worriers.

"He likes to keep to himself. Maybe he's one of those creative types, or he can't get around." That's Milton Kirkland's answer.

The regular convenience store clerk from noon till closing at nine PM tends to worry, but not too much. She makes a point of asking Darcy how her folks are. The girl always says fine. Darcy's folks have always been fine, and she can't see why that would have changed all of a sudden.

Darcy comes into the store.

"Hey!" says the clerk. "What can I do you for? How's the family?"

"Fine. I need some stamps. One." Darcy puts the envelope on the counter in the space between the cash register and a rack of different kinds of sugarless gum.

Mizez and Msr Fenner and Joe
Peter's Cotage
Kinggarden Ontereo

The clerk looks down at it, then asks, "You got a postal code?"

Darcy shakes her head and says, "I don't know what that is."

"An address?"

"No. It doesn't matter."

"What do you mean?"

"Everybody knows. You can ask for directions."

Darcy sounds so sure of herself that the clerk lets it go. She says, "Well, anything else for you?"

"Nope, thanks," says the almost seven-year-old.

The clerk tells Darcy how much the stamp is. Darcy carefully counts the money out, with only a little help. She takes the envelope from the counter, licks the stamp, sticks it on, and drops the envelope into the letterbox just outside the store.

Later, she drinks from the bottle of scotch she found in her cabin. She smokes a cigar. She draws a picture of her family and prints a story.

The scotch warms Darcy up. She is very focused on what she's doing. Everything is pleasant. The only thing bothering her is that she didn't bring any paints, markers, coloured pencils, or even crayons. She has to make do with no colour, only the plain grey HB pencils.

It gets dark, and Darcy is tired. She goes to bed. She dreams of her family on a car trip. She is crying in the dream, and her little brother, Joe, has motion sickness. Her mom keeps saying, "This will be fun!" Her dad curses and says, "Will you look at this so-called driving?"

In the dream, her mother asks her father if he wants a break. "I could take over," she says. He says, "I know what I'm doing, here," very quickly, as though he doesn't want to interrupt his running commentary about bad cars. In the dream, it occurs to Darcy that her dad thinks his constant complaints are somehow funny. Then Joe pukes.

She wakes up later than usual the next day. Darcy has a headache. She feels kind of sick. She goes to the kitchen table, where she left her dull drawing and story.

When she sees the story, Darcy can't take her eyes off it. Something changed near the end. One thing became another. After a while, she picks up the last page and takes it outside, still in her funky black, red, and white boys' PlayStation flannel pajamas. She's taken the time to put her coat and turtle boots on.

She goes to the convenience store and asks the clerk, "What is this?"

"Pardon?"

"What is this?"

"A&A Convenience?"

"No, this." Darcy shakes the page she's been holding up for the clerk.

"Well, dear. Is it something you did?"

"Yeah."

"Did you write it for me? Well, isn't that nice? Aren't you sweet? Did your mommy get you to write this for me?"

"What? Do what? You don't understand. I was asking you something." Darcy is upset. She leaves the store.

One of the other A&A regulars happens to be on her way to get some lactose-free milk. The girl and the woman recognize each other, and the woman, having lived her whole life in friendly Orchard Mines, says, "Good day."

Darcy says, "Hi. Um, could you help me?"

The woman says, "Why certainly, dear, what can I do for you?"

"Um," the girl says, "what is this?" She shakes the paper in front of the woman, who takes a look.

"It's part of a story. Did you write it?"

"What?"

"Did you write this, dear?"

"Why did you say that?"

"Say what, dear? I'm afraid I don't follow. Are you teasing me? I have a grandson about your age. Burtie. How he loves to tease his grammy! His grampy isn't around anymore really, so I let the little devil get away with more than I should. I wonder how things would be if Burtie had grown up with my Ted. . . ."

Darcy kicks pebbles with her turtled feet. The woman realizes she is rambling to a child. She always promises herself not to go on so much, and endlessly fails to keep that promise. "What I mean to say, dear, is did you write this?"

"Yup. But why are you saying that word?"

"What word, dear?"

"I know I can print, but you're saying, 'write.'"

"Oh, I see." The woman takes another look at the page. The lines are wobbly. Some of the words are hard to make out, and the spelling is pretty bad. "How do they teach you to spell these days?"

"No, it's not the spelling."

"Pardon?"

"You used the other word before."

"Oh, yes. Well, to be honest, it's a bit sloppy. I mean, there's lots of promise, dear. Don't give up! Never let anyone tell you to stop! I was –"

Darcy cuts in. "I'm not stopping. I just want to know what it is."

The woman is losing her patience. She is friendly, but she also needs her milk. She wants to get on with her day. And she doesn't appreciate rude, uncommunicative children. "Really, I am trying my best, but I cannot understand what you want from me, little lady."

Darcy takes the paper back. She decides to ask someone younger the next time. Someone who's old enough to figure it out, but close enough to her own age to know what she's talking about.

Down the street, there's a girl wearing a bright orange tank top with a big Hello Kitty on the front – a green bra strap showing – and flared blue tear-aways. Her yellow underwear is just visible above the waistline of her pants. Her running shoes are about a year out of date, but new. She is waiting by a pay phone that no one is using.

"Excuse me," says Darcy.

"Yeah," says the other girl.

"My name is Darcy and I'm wondering if you could help me."

"My name is Tina, and I'm bored shitless, so why not?"

The little girl blushes and feels shy. Finally, she says, "Uh, is this writing or printing?" Darcy gives Tina the page, but doesn't look at the older girl's face.

"Well, up here it's definitely printing, but this wobbly part could go either way."

Darcy says, "Are you busy now?"

Tina says, "That would be a massive negative. Why?"

For the next few nights, Tina and Darcy loop letters. They talk about the radical transformations of b, f, r, s, and z. They smoke and drink. Tina pops mints in her mouth so she won't get caught when she goes home. "I never thought this stuff was so much fun before," she says one time. "Never in a zillion years." She means language.

The letter arrives at the Peters' Cottage. Darcy's parents see the postmark of the little town where their daughter is staying. They cut their vacation short. They pack everything up into their shimmering silver suv, look at maps to choose their route, and drive north to find her. Darcy's mom makes up posters before they go.

Luckily, A&A is the only convenience store in Orchard Mines, and it's the first place where the family stops. When she gets inside, Darcy's mother asks, "Have you seen our daughter?" She is about to pull out a poster from her oversized tan-toned Roots satchel when the clerk answers.

"Sure, she was in here not twenty minutes ago. The mister's really going through them cigars, eh?" The clerk clears her throat and says quietly, "Should you really be letting her spend quite so much time with that Phipps girl?"

The mother is trembling. "Where is my baby? Where is my baby!" she says. Darcy's mother starts to hyperventilate.

The clerk pales. "Really, I'm sure the Phipps girl isn't any harm. I just mean with her reputation and all, I was –"

"Where is she?" The mother almost screams.

"Well, just by the Wilson place, of course. Your place."

The mother rushes out before she realizes she doesn't know where that is. She is both too embarrassed and too angry with the clerk to go back in. She does a few quick deep-breathing exercises to calm down. Her husband is in the idling car saying, "Honey? Honey?"

A man walks in their direction from the other side of the street. She shouts as friendly as possible at the man, "Excuse me, do you know where I can find the Wilson Place?"

"Sure thing. Just down that way on this street. Blue with blue trim, right on the corner before you get to Lakeview."

Darcy's mom gets in the car and her husband follows the directions. In no time, they are in front of the little cabin wrapped in dirty blue tarpaper made to look like brick.

When Darcy opens her door, the stale air coming out is powerful. She smiles at her mom and dad, who are standing on the porch. Her little brother, Joe, waits in the car with her healthy goldfish. She says, "I'm ready."

She gets her stuff. In the car, Joe doesn't pay attention to his family. He colours a story while talking to himself. He has gone over the same page so many times that it's now a muddy blob of browns and greys, with some bright coloured scales that were shed by the crayons clinging to the surface – red, yellow, purple, and green. He looks at the picture and says, half singing, to no one, "I have loved my sister since before she was born."

It

Look at the bats! Up there, look, bats."

"It's too early for bats."

"All I know is, look up."

The other boys come along. They crowd together and watch for bats. Sky. Bugs. Trees. A plane overhead. No one sees anything. John takes a stick, throws it in the air. Nothing. Some others throw little rocks up. Nothing.

John says, "So where are the bats, Crusty?"

The boy they call Crusty says, "They were just there."

"Yeah, right."

Some of the others say, "Yeah, right," too.

A smaller one pushes Crusty, who says, "Cut it out."

John says, "Hey, let's play one last game of super tag before it gets dark. Where's the gun?"

The gun is under the tree by Chris's cabin. Troy gets the gun. It's still full of water.

John says, "Troy, you're it."

Troy lets his arms dangle. He slouches, hunching his shoulders. His head dips and he says, "Oh," for a long time, making the sound go up at the end.

"Don't be a baby," John says.

"Fine," says Troy. He runs to the pole, turns his back to everyone. Covers his eyes and starts counting, "One . . . two . . . three –" really fast.

"Too fast!" Chris says.

Troy slows down a bit, and kicks the pole. He gets to twenty-four, twisting around before the number is fully out of his mouth. His arms cradle the gun when he's turning, but then he quickly lifts it into position.

"Twenty-five!" He opens his eyes. There stands Crusty, close enough to spit on. Troy says, "Not again," and runs around the other boy.

Crusty says, "No fair." Troy keeps running. Crusty lopes after him. "No fair," he says.

Troy is a good runner, so he gets away pretty easily. He spots Andrew, who realizes he's been seen. Andrew bolts. Troy closes in, but Andrew moves from side to side so he can't be tagged or shot at. Troy is waiting him out, watching for signs that Andrew is getting tired from running back and forth. He holds the gun at the ready. His upper body sways with the movement of the other boy. They are both laughing.

Andrew stops running. He has a stupid look on his face. Troy is disappointed that it'll be so easy. He thinks about finding someone else. Then he feels a hard pressure at the back of his legs and his knees give out. He is on the ground face down. He rolls over. Crusty stands above him.

Crusty says, "Shoot me."

Troy asks, "Why did you do that, you turd?"

"Shoot me!" says Crusty.

Andrew comes closer to the two others and says, "You're supposed to run away from the person that's it, not run *to* them."

"Just shoot me." Crusty's eyes glisten. His lips are getting thin.

Troy stays on the ground; his arms splayed out, slightly bent at the elbows. His right hand keeps a grip on the gun. He feels relaxed, almost happy.

Troy says, "I'm not shooting at anyone that's not running. Don't be so stupid."

Crusty runs around a bit, but nothing happens. Troy and Andrew are laughing now, in a mean way, at the other boy. "So, shoot me," says Crusty. "I'm running. Shoot me." He stops and says, "This is totally unfair, guys."

"You just don't even have a clue. This is so not how you play the game, you punk."

"I was running. For fuck's sake." Fuck isn't a word Crusty is used to saying. It comes out all funny from his mouth. The other boys start laughing even harder and meaner. Crusty gets an idea while they're not paying attention. He runs fast to Troy, lunging for the gun.

But Troy's grip is tight. Crusty has to pull hard, and he knows he's hurting Troy, a guy he knows everyone likes. He knows he'll pay for this, but he can't stop now. He gets the gun and starts shooting at his own self. He aims at his face and torso, pulling the trigger at close range. He is soaked. "I'm it. I'm it," he says.

"No you aren't," says Andrew. "This isn't the way to play. Don't be such a Crusty-head." Andrew tries to go for the gun, but he gets one in the ear. He curses and cringes, grabs at the injured side of his face. He says, "You're going to get it for that, even though it didn't hurt."

"I am it," says Crusty, "and I've got the gun to prove it."

"It's not even your Super Soaker, dude. Let's ask the guy who owns the gun what he thinks the rules are."

"I don't care, I have it and I am it."

"You can't be it if nobody plays," says Troy. "Didn't think of that, did you?"

Crusty is now officially very angry. He is almost shouting when he says, "No fair, no fair." Almost all the other kids playing the game are here now. They want to know what's happened. They are getting bored waiting to be chased, but they can also smell that something really good is about to happen. Chris arrives. John arrives. All the boys have arrived.

Troy says, "Chris, this is your Super Soaker. What do you say about a guy chasing the person that's it so he can be it?"

"What?" asks Chris.

"Yeah, exactly. Say you're it. Someone is chasing you, yelling, 'Shoot me, shoot me.' You don't shoot the guy and he pushes you down. He takes the gun and shoots himself."

"What?" asks Chris.

"Exactly. So, is this guy it now?"

"Is this for real?" asks Chris.

Another boy asks, "You let Crusty take the gun?"

Everyone is laughing while they make dum-dee-dum noises.

Crusty can't hold himself back anymore. He hollers, "What's the big deal? Why are you all acting this way? Why are you all so stupid to me? I want to be it, okay? So I want to be it. Let me be it!" He shivers because the evening has cooled off, even though the sun hasn't gone down all the way. It doesn't help that he is wet.

John is the one who will really make the decision. He's been listening with his arms crossed. He looks at Crusty and says, "You can't want to be it. That's just not the game. If you want to be it, you've got to act like you don't want to be it. You have to try hard not to get caught. Or then why have a game?"

"But why should I pretend?" Crusty is hardly even saying this out loud. He knows he's lost. He's crying a little bit, which all the boys knew would happen.

"It's too late to play now, anyway," John says. "The mosquitoes are coming out. Thanks for ruining yet another game, Cruddy."

They start to move away from each other. Crusty shoots at the other boys with the gun, but they run fast enough so that they only get a bit of water on their legs.

As he's getting away, Chris turns and says, "You better bring that back to my place tonight, or you are really really really going to get it."

There are a hundred red-tailed hawks over their heads right now, but none of the boys see them flying in great spirals, going from the tree tops up to where the human eye can't see. The low sun hits the feathers under their wings and on their bellies. None of the birds cry out. They twist, swirl to the west, and follow the sun to some destination. They are getting away from this country before it's too late.

Flat Earth

I t was April third. "Goodbye Yellow Brick Road" was the number five LP on the hit parade. Judy was on the Pink Panther, flying. She was nine, and the sky was a black-blue-grey. It was like nothing she had seen before. The wind was behind her, blowing strong against her back. Pushing her far down the suburban block.

There was no Motown coming out of open windows. Everything was tightly closed. No one else seemed to be outside. They were getting ready for what might come.

Judy, Pink Panther, flying.

The happiest of places: Windsor, 1974. Population around 190,000. Income for the family of six, maybe $10,000.

Pink Panther was a hand-me-down, but special. Pink and black. Name carefully lettered on the side. At one time there were streamers coming out of the handlebars. There were still some slightly faded bits of plastic sliding along the spokes making bright little *thik thik thiks* as she peddled. Other kids sometimes put cards in for their popping sound, but Judy didn't bother.

Judy didn't see the broad strokes of the bike's hand-done paint job. She didn't notice the rust. Whether it was too big or small was beyond her. Her dad had made it like new again, just for her. And so, she was in the perfect place, at the perfect time, on the perfect bike.

Forest Glade, Windsor, and the autoworkers were worried or unemployed. But did she notice? Did she think about OPEC or Watergate? Did she think about what critics said was behind those cute commercials with multicultural kids singing *Canada, we love thee*?

Did she even know about the FLQ?

Judy didn't like the Jackson Five, didn't like the Osmonds, couldn't understand her friends' crushes on *Seventeen* boys. She worried endlessly about whether she would ever get breasts, or whether she would always have a slight puffiness and aching to the left but nothing more.

A new McDonald's on Tecumseh. A new part of the subdivision about to be built. Another move just over a year away. None of these things mattered as the roof of the world came down low. And not in a bad way. The bruising clouds seemed to skitter just above the rooftops, bending saplings along the block. Judy on Pink Panther, unable to put her feet on the pedals for the force of the wind. It blew east, and so she flew. No hills or dips to slow her down. The road seemed to meet the horizon.

What clothes was she wearing? It was unseasonably warm, so draw your own conclusions. I can only tell you there were no glasses. She ran over her Cat's Eyes on the lonely man-made hill, behind the school at the end of grade three. The same grade she was in when a boy walked up to her, in line at the end of recess, and asked if she was a boy or girl. She was wearing a powder-blue halter-top, midnight-blue shorts, and her navy strap clogs. She wore a pixie cut her father had given her. She was wearing a lime-green banana harmonica hanging from a lime-green cord around her neck. She was standing beside her best friend, Barbara Suntz, who would soon move away.

Another time, on the longest day of the year, she was barefoot, hanging upside-down on the crossbar of the Lauzons' swing set. Memory keeps the coarse weave of her shorts, the knowledge that they must have been thick polyester, because everything was, and that the nut and bolt securing one swing's chain caught at the inseam that bright evening, causing a tear. The shorts were some soft pastel, and had nonsensical cuffs around the legs. Her hands were cool on the metal. She had the ridiculous sense that the day was never going to end, light as it was at nine at night. There was no sleepiness. No parent said, *Time for bed*.

But now, for this early evening, which was dark, dark, dark, no clothes exist for her. Judy was travelling west, or maybe east – anyway, down the block, far from home, fast, on her bike. It felt sometimes like the tires weren't even touching the sidewalk. Her heart was as alive as it would ever be.

She lived in a place where the kids were told, *Duck and Cover*. Not for a bomb, but for weather like this. Every spring, students were instructed to crouch down and press their bodies against particular cinderblock walls in school. To curl up to walls that would stand. Go to a basement if there was one. Hide under something very heavy. Try not to use anything electrical. Listen to the radio for when it's safe. Winds can exceed 200 miles per hour. Most fatalities happen when people don't leave mobile homes or automobiles.

Outside here, the sky was taking her, though; it's not so hard to understand. Seeing it, she was taken by the sky, like a woolly grey blanket edging past the map's four corners. Feeling it, she became part of it, as the wind pushed her beyond house after house after red brick and aluminum siding model house. Going down Esplanade Drive, quick quick, away from her own home.

The Lauzons were inside, the Lees were inside, and the

Smiths were somewhere else and separate, having just gotten their divorce. Only Judy, Pink Panther, the flat earth, and the sky. But after the long euphoria, she knew it was time to head back, and turned around to the force that now blew against her.

We were all new here. We were all from someplace else. My family was one of the first on the two model streets built to lure others. Roots were only a matter of months or at most a couple of years. I was one of the original Brownies in what is now known as the Forest Glade District Girl Guides, Kanata Division, in the Trillium area. I don't remember seeing a Trillium in Windsor.

My father's Presbyterian Church held services in the public-school library. Two of my siblings were shipped off to other schools I could barely fathom, out there . . . downtown, miles away. They even had to take different buses. One of my brothers was in the same school as I was, but he was Older, and couldn't show he knew me when we passed in the halls. Otherwise he'd be a wimp or something.

As of Tuesday, April second, the Jackson Five was number two with "Dancing Machine." Michael Jackson wasn't cute. Something about him bugged Judy. There was something fake. What was a little kid doing, singing about love and heartbreak? What was a child doing with a fuzzy pink hat and heels like that? Who was dressing him up like so? But he could sing, that's for sure. The next week, the Jacksons be number-one on CKLW's "Hit Parade." So what? The radio station was in Windsor, but it wasn't really about the place at all, her dad said. It played James Brown, the Pips, and Alice Cooper. But the government had to make CKLW – "The Big 8" – play Joni Mitchell or Gordon Lightfoot. Canadian Content was the only thing to get "Sundown" on once in a while. That was according to what her dad said.

However, this was Wednesday, after school, April third, 1974, on Esplanade Drive, a model street of a Wimpey Construction Company-built subdivision, this side of vegetables grown for Green Giant and endless sweet-smelling tobacco grown for Macdonald's Exports and other cigarettes.

The sky was underlined pea green . . . was a simmering purple . . . was slate lined with a sickly yellow and Judy turned against it. She stood up on her bike and pushed a pedal with all her might. She felt the wind sculpt her, bite into her legs. Her left foot, higher up, was not coming down. Her lips pulled back in concentration. A lot of people confused this look with a smile, so they thought she was nicer than she actually was. This often served her well.

She pushed and got nowhere. The wind became stronger and the sky fell some more. To top it off, night was coming. She was a bit of an adventurer, but this was scary. Her hands gripped white. Her foot ached for the pushing.

Then her mother, Ruth, came into view.

She wore a dress that went down to mid-thigh. No belt. She wore flat shoes. Her brown hair was shorter than the fashion of the time dictated for a woman her age. She smiled like Buddha. Ruth was calling, but could not be heard. Only the wind came from her mouth. As she came closer, lips moved, *Judy, come home.*

Along the street, it was the same story. Everybody came from someplace else. Vaughan's dad was a boxer from Detroit or maybe Chicago. I can't remember anything about his mom except she was pretty. Vaughan was cute, looked a little like Michael J. Across the street from us, Tommy Lee had the biggest collection of K-Tel records. He was the only kid in his family who was born in China, before the Cultural Revolution, before his mom the opera singer had to leave. It took me years to figure out she sang like the records that she played when her friends came over to play mah-jong. That she sang Chinese opera, not the stuff the fancy neighbours next door listened to on CBC radio Saturday mornings.

Home is here, in my head. It's a Wimpey-built model house from which the siding peeled off on the first windy day. Where water fell like Niagara through the living room's bay window when it rained. My sister punched a hole in her bedroom wall. This building is blessed with my first real sense of being.

Judy, come home. And she tried. Ruth turned to walk to the house, then looked behind her to see her daughter stuck in amber. The mother came back, right up to Pink Panther. She took hold of the handlebars and pulled. The bike moved, with Judy hard on the pedals, trying to help.

Together, mother and daughter inched along the sidewalk. Judy, Ruth, and Pink Panther, crawling. Judy was wrapped up in the drama, feeling her breath being whipped from her mouth. Ruth was too aware of the danger; she put all her effort into being calm, looking as though this was an everyday thing. *Not to worry.* This was Ruth's talent, her unseeable skill. The calm of the storm.

My father is from Windsor. He was born there just in time to welcome the Depression. His father owned Sandy MacDonald's Garage. By the time my dad was four and a half, he could be blindfolded and tell one car from another, just sitting there on the curb, listening to them go by.

> The Essex . . .
> the De Soto . . .
> the La Salle . . .
> and there was always the cheeky rattle of the
> Chevrolet.

Around the same time, his dad, Sandy, lost the garage. The family moved to Stratford. It was tough on everyone's pride. But my dad still remembers how well his father fixed cars. How smart and practical he was with metal things. It's a big deal, especially in a place like Windsor.

Dad doesn't talk much about growing up. Neither does my mom, Ruth, who was also born in 1929.

The dress I remember my mother wearing on that stormy day is a dress found in a black-and-white picture. It's our family, standing in front of the vw Bug we had in Guyana (a car we wouldn't have dreamed of owning in a town that belonged to the Big Three). I'm the baby in my mother's arms.

Because of the picture, I know the grade-four storm memory is wrong, that Ruth MacDonald wouldn't have worn the same clothes almost a decade later. It wouldn't have been practical to bring a dress all the way to Canada, or to lug it and four children across the country when we moved from Saskatoon to

Edmonton to this city of Windsor. But there she is, walking up to me, dressed in history, and for some reason I can't explain, it feels like my heart might break.

The wind roared in their ears, so they laughed without hearing each other. And slowly, slowly, Ruth and Judy got home. On this special day, Pink Panther came in too, so the weather couldn't take him away.

The TV was on, the image washed with snow, fuzzy greys with some dialogue and song breaking through the static every once in a while. Her brothers and sister were there. Judy sat down. Together, they watched flying monkeys and a little dog. Some strange crew of misfits trying to find something. Judy was told this was a special movie. That it was one of the first made with brilliant colour. Their TV was black and white.

She was told she should like this movie because the star shared her first name.

The family lived in the land of flat. And as they tried to see wonder through the atmospheric interference – the thick dust kicked up by the storm – a tornado touched down nearby. Earlier, others had visited as far away as South Carolina. In Michigan, the very same severe weather rushing through Windsor now had already caused flash flooding, wind gusts, and a series of tornadoes. Three people died there, two in mobile homes. Windsor's pancake surface made it easy for a storm to run along. The Detroit River topping it, and the lakes on either side, gave bad weather a second wind.

In my city, the funnel's tip caressed the top of a curling club then moved on, taking the roof with it. Nine people died. Thirty were injured. The following Sunday, a neighbour came to the church in the library, bruised and shaken. Her leg was swollen, an indigo black and violet blue. She wore shorts and couldn't move so well. She had been curling that night. Some of her friends had died. The same roof had fallen on her. But here she was, in Forest Glade Public School. In Forest Glade subdivision. In Windsor, Ontario, April, 1974.

Work

J enny and Manjula were friends. They were going to the mall in their new dresses. They wore sensible pumps, ready for a lot of walking. The mall was on the edge of town, so they got on the bus and sat at the back.

Jenny and Manjula didn't like the front of the bus. The seats faced the aisle on either side, and other people scuffed shoes as they went by. At the front, there was also a chance they'd have to stare at strangers staring right back. And strangers do the rudest things, even with the driver so near.

There were disadvantages to sitting at the back, though. One of them was sitting two seats in front of them. An old man twisted around to face them, mouthing what Jenny and Manjula knew were lewd words as he stared at their breasts.

The man had that translucent skin some men get, so you're surprised when you brush against their faces and they have whiskers. You can't imagine a beard growing on something so fragile. He also had silky white hair, combed back and sharply cut. He looked like a fairytale English grandfather fresh from a military exercise, or an s&m parlour.

He went from silent words to something worse. Jenny and Manjula didn't know exactly what worse. But his chin started to jut up and down, his arms stiff at his sides, his hands hidden. His eyes all over them.

Jenny had had enough. She hissed, "Let's get off." Neither

girl was aware that the next stop was for the shopping mall any-way.

The old man really threw Manjula. She saw the shopping mall right there on the other side of the road, but she thought that maybe Jenny knew something she didn't. Before she had a chance to really think things through, she remained seated while her friend stepped off. Manjula bolted to the door just as it was closing and the bus was pulling away. Too late. She would have to wait for a while because, out here, there was more space between stops. That meant a long walk.

Manjula felt miserable. It was so hot, and there was no side-walk, and the road was very grimy. She looked down at her pumps with their modest heels. Such a rich pumpkin colour and not one scratch – they would be ruined by walking all the way to the mall, or at the very least, they'd finally look *worn*. And she would be hot and tired and in no frame of mind to shop or even look around.

Manjula pulled the cord and threw herself back into the seat. She wondered whether Jenny would still go to the mall. Manjula wondered whether Jenny would wonder why Manjula hadn't got off, too. Manjula was sort of mad at Jenny, but she didn't really know why.

Finally, the next stop came. Manjula got off and started walk-ing back. She started sweating almost right away. It was even hot-ter than she'd remembered, maybe because the bus's air condi-tioning had been blasting down her neck.

There was a gas station. It wasn't for regular people needing to top up before going to the corner store, but for people who *work* in their vehicles. An oily smell drifted by. The garage dog was filthy and chained to a rotting unpainted little house turned grey by the sun. The dog looked at her and made some limp barks.

The air was dense with dust. As she walked, it became clear where the plume came from.

Stretched across the road, a huge flatbed truck was butted up against a much smaller dump truck. The flatbed was the biggest rig Manjula had ever seen. She hadn't noticed it from the bus because she was thinking about Jenny and looking at her hands so that she could blank out the old man. Now she thought, *Jeez, I'm gonna have to walk around this thing to get to the mall. I'm gonna have to go right onto the road. Stupid thing. Hope there's no cars.*

Then Manjula noticed it wasn't just dust. The closer she got, the larger the pieces were that came down. She looked around to find out why. The top of the truck's bed was so high that the sun's rays jabbed into her eyes. It took a while to focus, and even then the image was all black against the bleached-out, burning sky.

Up there, she saw a man throwing what looked to be huge slabs of concrete from the flatbed into the dump truck. It seemed ridiculous, that a man should be doing something so pointless, blocking her from getting to the mall for who knows how long. Was she supposed to just stand there and wait till he was done? She couldn't get by, she saw, because maybe, with everything that was flying around, she would get hit. Surely, a driver or someone would notice her and move one of the trucks to let her go. Or maybe at least the man she saw would stop for a bit.

Manjula stepped back, crossed her arms. The lemon-yellow rayon dress she'd picked out to go shopping in fluttered with the breeze a little. She wasn't thinking, or she wouldn't have crossed her arms and risked creasing the dress across her chest. But she wanted to make a point. She wanted to look official and threatening – or at least annoyed – if one of the workers happened to see her there. Manjula anchored her weight on her left leg, allowing the right to come forward with her toes pointed out. She'd seen ads with businesswomen standing the same way. It was kind of official.

Fifteen, twenty minutes went by. No one noticed her. She was sure she was being insulted. Manjula was starting to feel the old ache when she'd been frustrated for long enough that she was just about to cry. She started to droop. She looked up again to distract herself. She didn't want to cry here.

The man up at the top of the truck was still doing what she'd seen him do before. But now it was clear he'd taken off his t-shirt. The sun lit up streams of sweat fighting against the dust and grime of his work. He swiveled his torso right to left, picking up a slab, pulling it to him, shifting his weight and tossing the slab onto the other truck, doing this again and again. Manjula remembered being told this was not a good way to lift – that you should bend at the knees and keep your back straight. Without really thinking about why, she started to worry.

For who knows how long, Manjula watched him work. His motions were repetitive, but he was in no way like a machine. He worked rhythmically, with smooth movements back and forth. Over the growling sounds of the trucks' idling motors, Manjula heard the man's throaty grunts, now that she really listened.

Ribbons of sweat marked his muscles. He seemed so much a part of his work that strain and discomfort were not obvious in his movements. He didn't complain. His body was his work, and that was all. Manjula thought of beauty, squinting against the sun, as small bits of concrete rained down on her. The work's purpose was not the point.

After a while, there was finally a lull in all the motion and noise. The trucks' motors were shut off and the worker seemed to be taking a break. His arms rested still and straight against his sides.

Manjula smiled as she shouted, "Hey! Hey! Hey, you up there, you were amazing. What you're doing is amazing! What are you doing?"

"What?" he said. "What am I doing?"

"It's amazing," she said.

"It's work. I'm just working, you know? It's just what I have to do, that's all." His voice was flat, and maybe it was choked with dust from the concrete because it had a dry sound. "What are you doing here, that's what I'd like to know. What're you doing in the middle of nowhere, dressed like that?"

"I kind of got lost," she said.

"I'll say." He turned away from her and sat down, still on the flatbed. From somewhere he took out a thermos of syrupy black coffee. He opened it, then poured some coffee into a plastic cup.

The trucks didn't move, so Manjula went around them, watching out for cars squeezing by. She walked slowly, hoping that he might talk to her again.

Terrazzo

S he's sixteen, and every day she goes through the same ritual. During lunch hour, she sits in front of her locker eating a bag of Hostess barbecue potato chips and drinking Sealtest chocolate milk.

She sits there, her legs sprawled across the cold and polished floor, her locker open. Books are neatly slotted side by side on the top shelf, and pictures of horses and dogs line the inside of the door. There's a memo board with an erasable marker surface, featuring Ziggy and his dog waving from the sidelines. On it she has drawn a lightly shaded purple heart. There are no messages, except for Ziggy's manufactured words.

The girl is plump. Kids in her class whisper hotly after they walk by her, saying she's too loud and pretends to be somebody. They cackle about her boldly coloured clothes with chunky patterns that make her look even fatter than she is.

In the change room after gym class, she talks about her father. His dull attention suffocates. Her mother is a saint, she says, but with no real conviction. The others concentrate on bra straps, baby powder, the lines of their lips. After a while, the popular girl fixes glazed eyes on that figure and wonders, as her gaze slides by, if someone is crazy to talk to themselves, or if it's true *only* if they answer. The rest of the girls lower their heads, concealing smiles of conspiracy.

She is alone, listening to echoes of the others at play. Once in a while two seniors neck four lockers down from hers. They never say hello.

And every day – every day during her stay at high school, for five years – she sits by her locker clamping the chips between her back teeth, with her mouth slightly opened so the grinding can be heard far down the hall. She sucks intently on a straw. A book might be propped up in front of her, a convenient decoy. This is a duty. A sacrament.

Later, she goes to university, then breaks down. Returns home. Stops eating.

The same communion cannot suffice, will not sustain, does not brush her lips. Kissing death briefly, she is corrected and returned. Conversation is about the furtive series of lovers she had while away, and talk of how she became so good at second-guessing the shrinks, she got to their points before they did. Freudians wanted to know about sex, and her father.

A job comes along, working with horses. She falls in love with a woman there. She dates a boy, knowing it is expected.

When a former schoolmate comes to visit (who now lives in the large city), the favourite topic is the other high-school girls moving back home from university. They have all gained weight. None of them know what to do. All of them talk to her now, in this small town. Playing volleyball at night in the old school gym, they ask her about diets to follow. She is finally part of the game.

In two years' time, she says, she would like to get married (but not especially to the guy she's with). This is her plan: if there are to be no nuptials, she'll go back to the books, get a degree. Maybe become a teacher just like dad.

Grinding molars crack and cry through the night, when she's alone, thirsting for some water or some wine.

Happy Days

She didn't know too much about him in the beginning, so everything was perfect. He said he liked her hair and that they were soul mates. They didn't go too far too fast the first few days, but there was a lot of heat, a strong connection. They talked about when they might have kids. She wanted so badly for this to be something meant to be.

They spent all of the next four days together. She had asked him over for tea and he didn't leave. They talked till their heads ached. They held hands. They slept together with clothes on. The groceries ran low, but they didn't go shopping. They had little quarrels and grew light-headed. They finally had intercourse, then they fought. She loaned him some money. He went home. She met a friend at a coffee shop, saying, "This is finally it."

A couple of nights after that, she went over to his place. She saw Treasure Trolls along the landing up to the apartment. They also lined bookshelves and a desk. She saw dinosaur models strung from the ceiling. She saw an Elvis bust on a giant empty cable spool in the cramped living room. He had a *Star Trek* poster on the wall. There were dozens of big collapsed boxes piled on one side of the dining room.

"When did you move in?" she asked.

He answered, "Two years ago."

"Are you planning to move again soon?" She was wondering

whether it would be too fast for them to live together. She thought it might be.

He said, "No, no plans to move."

A week after that, she was talking with her friend about the happy days, saying how right everything was at the start, even though it was obvious to her now that he was a bit of a psychopath. After those first four days, he said he could take or leave sex, and that he didn't really need it. He didn't pay the loan back. He gave her a yeast infection. He had sex with someone else and told her. A month later, she left him one last message, which he didn't return.

MESSAGE RECEIVED JULY 24, 1998, 10:48 PM

I am back in the city. I was in Joliette, having the time of my life. The people there were less hypocritical and not so phony and fake. But I missed you, even though you might think it's funny. I hope to see you, even though you might think it's funny.

If you walk towards me, I will help you. If you walk away from me, I will help you. I don't see why there is any problem. If you do, I guess I won't be hearing from you.

It was very very nice to meet you. And I really don't understand why you didn't find me acceptable, but that's the way life goes. I think we really really could have been a hit. So I do this, again, so as not to disturb you, not to bring any uncomfortableness in your life intentionally or unintentionally.

But you're a sweetie and a cutie when you want to be as well as an intelligent individual. You have some control issues. I think that's what it's about with your eating and with me. I've read about that. I could have helped you, but oh well. God bless.

No one's ever done this to me. No one. I thought you loved me, but obviously you can't love anyone. Obvious to everybody except me, I guess. Well, you taught me that lesson that's for sure. Goodbye. Have a good life.

He didn't know what she meant about the eating. He saved the message. When he got back from drinking with buddies some nights, he would play it through a few times. He stroked the phone. He imagined walking onto a streetcar and seeing her again. She would tell him what to do, making sense of everything. She would make him feel small and stupid, but things would be so much better after that. During the day, he made a point of taking unusual routes.

There is No Year Zero

A little cuckoo sound and it's time to cross the street. They are holding hands, not watching out for cars. Not making sure things are safe. Ruby looks down. She sees –

carrots
beans
tampons
rice
soap
tomatoes

A list that makes her think of the tricky "e." A book says that, when he was vice president of the United Sates, Dan Quayle told a kid, "You've got it right phonetically, but you're missing a little something." It's a pretty famous story, but some people think the former vice president wrote it on a blackboard or somehow spelled it out loud. That's not right, if you believe the book. Instead, he saw the word, and the word was potato, written down in a child's hand. And Dan Quayle – almost-leader of the free world – hinted to the kid that it could maybe use an "e" at the end. Potatoe.

Ruby knows that shopping lists can show stuff the writer didn't mean to show. It's so rare to write things down, once you reach a certain age and don't have school assignments. Lists are all some people have as their own record, not a government one. Something that shows what they want, what they dream of, what their plans are. Not an official thing to be processed by. That kind of stuff just shows how you fit in. Or don't.

eggs

Ruby writes a lot of things down. She's trying to be more in touch with her creative side and also be more practical. She has read *The Artist's Way*. She has a dream journal and a daily journal and even a special little book to list the things she needs. She is looking at that now as she crosses the street with her boyfriend.

Cuckoo. Cuckoo.

The warning is spaced out. She can't even hear it. She doesn't hear the traffic. A police car goes by, its siren whooping halfway through the intersection. Ruby doesn't slow down or look up. She is too caught up in the list. She is missing something.

whole wheat flour
soba noodles
gluten

She is barely holding hands with Andy, only he doesn't go by Andy. Ever since he moved from home a couple of years ago, he's told people to call him Rep, or Repo, but nobody calls him Repo. Rep is hungry, so it's not a good time to shop, which is what they plan to do, because Ruby said she had to, and Rep said he didn't care. He is spaced out, looking at the clouds and the ground. There is no view.

guava juice
sucanat
mangoes

Ruby looks at the "e." She remembers what else she read in a joke book – that former U.S. vice president Dan Quayle also supposedly said the Holocaust was something terrible that happened this century, that we're all from this century and that he was not from this century. He was talking about the twentieth century, and he was speaking during it. But maybe he wasn't from it. Maybe he had a good point. She gets back to the list, thinking about how lucky she is to have so much to choose from. She likes the clothes from the sixties and seventies, but she's happy to have more than granola and bean sprouts to buy.

sesame crackers
oyster sauce
tempeh

Ruby dreamt last night about one of her brothers chasing the rest of the family around with an axe. She woke up when he hunkered over her, hands clasped tight against the wood of the handle, arms thrown behind his back, now coming down on her in a full-force swing. She didn't put this one in her dream journal. She got up and did some I Ching. The Earth below, The Mountain above. *Po.* Collapse.

The Disposable Heroes of Hiphoprisy said, "The only cola I would support is a cost of living allowance." Ruby doesn't drink cola. Even the word sounds strange to her. She doesn't know what the band was talking about, either. When she first saw it on the countdown of the best videos of the millennium, she thought theirs was okay. Rep likes it way more.

Ruby has a really boring job in an office. She can't do her hair exactly how she wants. She can only put in colour that washes out by Monday. So she's pretty normal looking and she's not really part of the group they hang with. Their friends call her a conformist. Meanwhile, Rep is as cool as they come – the right shirts, shoes, hair, attitude. He won't read books because they're too bourgeois. Ruby writes –

>Potatoes
>fucking potatoes.

Rep and Ruby have been going out for a while, but they don't live together. Friends wonder about this, too. Her hair, her job, and what they're holding out for. Their friends think Ruby is both too status-quo-zombie-dead-grown-up and not grown-up enough to go ahead with an obvious thing. Scared like a little girl. Not that living together is really much of anything anymore. Way too many parents seem to think it's a practical first step, including her own. First step to being what they are – something Ruby isn't really interested in. But anyway, it *is* something. Living together is not just being roommates, and it's definitely not like being with parents or living in a shallow basement apartment in Scarborough alone, which she is.

What Ruby and Rep do is none of their friends' business: the couple can say this to each other as many times as they want. But it actually does eat away at them. And the more time that passes, the less sure Ruby and Rep are that they want to live together. Not that they really talk about it. Not in detail.

The thing is, Rep's mother just died. So the couple went back to his hometown, and he was Andy again. Andy without a mom. When she was alive, he mostly didn't talk about her. And when he did talk about her, it was all how she put him down, put his dad down, expected too much, said really hurtful things about people.

But being back in his hometown, called a name Ruby didn't know at all, this guy just kept on saying, "I won't get a chance to show her. She won't get a chance to see me make it." Like that was the whole point of his mom's life. Back in the place where he grew up, Rep AKA Andy tried not to have sex in his parents' house. Kept talking about sacrilege, even though back on Planet Anarchy he's always talking it up about not believing in God.

Even since they finally came back to the city, they haven't really done it. A couple of times, after they went partying, it got to heavy petting, but then Rep pulled away. They've slept in the same bed sometimes, but far apart. One might touch the other's cheek or thigh, but soft and quick, like good parents do with kids.

Ruby has been checking her list since she and Rep left his shared downtown house about twenty minutes ago. She's checked it over and over. She scratched things out and added other stuff. She fixed any bad spelling. She even wrote out the list a couple of times when she decided it was too sloppy. She goes through what she needs, again and again. Looking down. Not looking around her.

Ruby and Rep are almost across the grey wet shitty street. When they get to the curb, they nearly walk right into a guy waiting to cross the other way. At the last second, the couple swerves to avoid him. Without thinking about it, Rep grabs Ruby's arm to guide her. Ruby would complain, but at least it's something. At least it's some kind of touch that shows he knows she's there.

Rep says, "Careful."

Ruby says, "Yeah, right. Thanks. What a help."

Rep looks hurt and Ruby's sorry. But he really is bugging her ass, too. She's frustrated because she wants sex, although not really with him if she lets herself think about it. But she's with him, and he doesn't want it.

Since Rep heard that his mother died, they've done it once, in his parents' house. Something took over that had never been there before. They were sleeping in the living room, on different couches. Other relatives were in the spare rooms. Not that the house was so big in the first place. Rep – Andy – would get under Ruby's covers for a little while and then go back to where he was sleeping. He would talk about his mom and how much he missed her. He talked about his dad and how everyone else was letting the old guy down. Andy would cry, and Ruby would hold him.

After a couple of nights like this, something changed. The funeral happened. The man at the front got the mother's name wrong. All these people came over, had coffee and cakes, talked about what a wonderful woman she was, how she would be missed. So many people in wools, they gave off a weird kind of steam. So many pinkies sticking out from cup handles. But they all finally left, and after a few heavy sighs and hands across his teary eyes, the father said he'd go lie down.

"I fall into myself," he said. "I don't sleep, but I get lost somehow. I can't really tell you. I'm always thinking about her. How she was before she wouldn't wake up. The last time she looked at me." He didn't say what he meant about the look. It had been so full of hate; thinking about it made his knees weak. "It's heart rendering," he said. "Heart rendering,"

About half an hour after his dad left, Andy came over to Ruby's couch. The leather squeaked a bit under the sheet. They looked at each other with try-to-be-quiet faces. When Andy got under the covers and touched her arm, electricity shot through Ruby. She had a sense that Andy felt the same thing. They held each other closer than they had the other nights. He breathed softly into her ear, and his breath got deeper. Slow and loud and it made her want him bad.

They were lying on their backs on the fancy green leather couch. She turned her head and licked his ear, like a cat. Not messy. She tickled his earlobe with her tongue. He jerked his head away, but pulled her tight at the same time. Andy turned on his side, and Ruby could feel he was hard under his pajama bottoms.

"I miss her, Ruby," he said.

"Yeah," she said.

"I don't know why I feel this way," he said. "You feel so good right now. I don't know why I feel like this."

"It happens, I guess. I hear sometimes it makes you really appreciate being alive or something."

"Yeah. This is different."

They were lying pretty still for a while. Every surface was tingling. The smallest move sent a shock through Ruby's body. She had never felt like this before. They were moving their hands under each other's pajamas, slowly in circles. They faced each other, their noses touching. They were so close everything was blurry.

Ruby felt waves. It was like her skin was melting. She was opening up and disappearing at the same time. They kissed lips, rubbed each other's back.

Andy said, "I love you."

He asked, "What's happening?"

She said, "Don't worry," and, "It's okay." "You're going to be okay," she said. And she really meant it. She didn't know what she meant.

She was getting into him. Everything he did and didn't do felt right. Andy touched her crotch and she was so wet, her nightie was soaked right through in that spot. He pulled the nightie up and drew little circles on her clit, not too hard, like hardly any guy knew how to. She put her hand down his pajama pants and stroked his cock. Firm but not squeezing. Going down behind his balls, cupping them and rolling them.

They stayed so quiet. They listened to every creak in the house. But they were so far away. It was such a struggle to re-member what the situation was. It was like they were both glow-ing, like they were both caught in some kind of awesome light only the two of them could see. They were so close together, and with their clothes pushed up and down it didn't take much for Andy to be inside. They weren't being safe.

Ruby got on top. They barely had to move before she came. She had to remember not to get into it the way she usually did because of where they were. Somehow, not shouting, "Oh God," or whatever made it more intense. The feeling of everything melting away kept growing, even after she came. Andy pushed from underneath. They were cupping each other's face. She could feel his cock deep inside. She could feel his stomach mus-cles tighten and relax. She felt like she was inside him, fucking herself, felt like she was going to come again, which she did. Then Andy pulled out and came, too.

They held each other close, but didn't say a word. Breathing sweetly into each other's ear. And she knew this was it. The end and the beginning.

The next day, when she was in the bathroom for a while, she found a book about stupid things politicians say, mostly quotes from the States. Dan Quayle seemed to be the winner.

A few days after that, they left Andy's hometown to come

back to the city. Now he's Rep again, but Rep with a new angel mother hovering just above him, watching everything he does from here on in. Rep not touching Ruby.

e

Pedestrians listen for the chirp-chirp sound and look for the light. They cross the street. Ruby adds this one last item. She puts it on the list. She thinks about the century she's walking into, and about turning back.

"Want to move in together?" she asks, and Rep says, *K*.

The Collection

In the playground of the Catholic school, a man in a motorized wheelchair. Children riding bikes in front of him. Older boy, little girl on pink bike. Both wear helmets. Going in circles. They crash. The little girl really wipes out and cries for her mom. The boy looks sad and sorry. The man touches a switch and goes to her.

She runs away, leaving her bike on the stale old asphalt. She calls, "Mommy!"

The man follows her around. He says, "Come on." He asks, "What do you want me to do?" She keeps running, crying. He starts to laugh with frustration. She looks at him, angry now, running. Then she starts to laugh.

She comes to him. He goes to her. She throws her arms onto his lap. He strokes her helmet.

They laugh together.

The older boy watches, kicking at the girl's bike, afraid he'll be blamed for everything. He doesn't ease up with all the laughter. She scraped her knee in the accident. Her pants are ruined with blood and a hole. Their mother isn't in on the joke.

They go home. The older boy guides both bicycles along. The girl holds the man's free hand. When they arrive back home, they see that the grandparents are there on a surprise visit.

The mother sees the girl limping, the ruined pants. She looks fiercely over to the older boy, but can't get mad in front of her own parents, especially when this is the first time they are meeting her new boyfriend. And he was with the kids. Responsible.

The grandfather says, "We heard you just had number six, Todd. Happy birthday!" He hands over a set of brand-new shiny 1976 Montreal Olympic coins with a face value of two hundred dollars.

The coins are individually wrapped in plastic and nestled in a blue velvet inlay with sized indents for each one. The case is wrapped in a rich brown Naugahyde that sports a gold embossed Olympic stamp on the lid, and a little lock with a little key.

The grandfather says, "Take good care of that. It's an investment. It'll be worth something some day."

Todd says thanks in a gush. He's not all that excited about the coins, but he knows that this unplanned trip by his grandmother and grandfather, and his birthday, and the stress of pulling together a meal tonight will mean that his mother will forget about the limp and the pants.

His sister seems fine, anyway. Is already making faces at him when she knows nobody is looking. Todd will be seeing chewed peas on her tongue tonight during supper. Maybe she'll laugh and choke on them.

Todd is twenty-six. He tried university but didn't like it, so he left. It seemed boring and beside the point. He lives in a place, then moves to try out another one. He writes to the folks he meets, and they write back, because his letters are a delight. He draws on envelopes and clips news stories about owls running amok or mice becoming friends with cats. He includes the photos with the news. He slips them in the envelopes with his thoughts about the world – like how free cheddar cheese would make people get along better.

Todd is very broke. He is back in the city where he grew up, back at his dad's apartment for a visit, sleeping on the living room floor. He's been here two weeks, and hasn't done what he came here to do.

His mom lives closer to downtown, in a nice house with her second husband, the boyfriend from the bike accident. Todd usually wants to stay with them. Better food and a happier place to hang out. But his father is going through a lot of bad luck, is depressed and needs the company because his friends avoid him. He's getting chemo but can't quit the cancer sticks.

Also, being so broke, Todd wouldn't know what to say to his mom and stepdad right now. He'd be afraid that his mom would see his father in him. He's afraid that his stepdad would finally try to give him a talk about being a man.

Todd is also being practical. All his extra stuff is socked away in his father's storage unit, and he can't just ask for the keys to it without spending some quality time.

He's come here to try and scare up some money.

The green grass around the bank is grey through the building's floor-to-ceiling tinted glass.

Todd waits in the lineup. He had all day to come here, but didn't plan well. It's lunchtime. Many customers with questions, with hands full of bills, and cheques, and desperation.

He gets his turn. Pulls the case out of a plastic shopping bag. Todd lays the rich Naugahyde down in front of the teller. He

71

asks, "How much can I get for this?"

The teller says, "Well, just a moment." She sees the Olympic rings embossed in gold on the top. She opens the case. She likes the feel of the velvet inside.

When the case is open, she says, "Two hundred dollars."

Todd says, "Two hundred dollars? It can't be two hundred dollars. It was two hundred dollars twenty years ago."

"And it's two hundred dollars now, sir."

"But it's a collector's item. It's a set. There's got to be some sort of appreciation or whatever."

The teller says, "I'm sorry, but it's two hundred dollars. That's what I see here."

"They're in mint condition, too! Look how each one is wrapped. Not one scratch."

She says, "I'll give you two hundred dollars for the set."

Todd says, "What about the case? The case is in great shape. What do I get for the case?"

"You get nothing for the case," says the teller.

"You've gotta be kidding."

"No, I'm sorry, I'm not. Policy."

Todd says, "Okay, then." He starts to pull the coins out from the blue velvet inlay, which he now sees is really cheap fluff stuck onto the plastic inlay form.

She asks him what he is doing. She says, "The coins go with the case. It's a set. You're wrecking it."

Todd says, "Yes, it is a set. But you don't want to pay for the set. You don't want to pay any extra for the case, so you don't get it. Two hundred bucks gets you the coins, that's it."

Todd gets his two hundred dollars and the case.

He walks back to his father's place, trying to think about where he'll get more cash. He takes the case out of the plastic bag. He wonders what he can do with it. He opens it. He runs his fingers back and forth across the cool soft surface of the fake velvet inlay.

The Europeans

A few years after moving away from home, I noticed this bird landing beside some dried-out bread someone had thrown on a little fenced-in front yard in downtown Toronto. Just after the bird came down, clicking and whirring, three or four others joined it. These birds eating bread all clicked and whirred and whistled. I liked the sound, even though you couldn't call it pretty. It was as if they were talking. I also noticed that their feathers were really shiny, making them look almost like they were made of metal. Their colouring was mostly black, with bits of brown, creamy white, and rust red flecked through. When the sun hit them, the black turned into a shimmering slate blue. They had long, narrow, yellow beaks, flat brown eyes, short tails, and sweet stocky bodies on sweet skinny legs. They were about the same size as a robin.

A little later, I was in Queen's Park at the beginning of fall. Shadows and light have an edge in the afternoon at that time of year. It was still warm out this particular day. I was walking around with friends; all of a sudden, I heard a really strange sound. In the city, there's hardly ever a chance to hear a lot of the same animals in one place. But all around me, above me, getting inside me, was that clicking and whirring, hundreds of times over. It drowned out the sound of the cars driving around the park.

I don't know why, I got really excited. "Do you hear that, do you hear that?" I kept saying.

My friends looked at me and said, "Yeah."

"Holy shit, there must be thousands of them."

They didn't say anything. Every so often, a few dozen birds came out of the trees, flew around, and went back into the crisp, fall leaves.

"Do you know what kind they are?"

Everyone shrugged. No one knew, or cared. They just knew they were nasty ugly birds.

"They must be getting ready to migrate," I said. "Good luck!"

"You're touched," one friend said.

A while later, my parents came to visit. We went for a walk, and saw one of these birds. Not that my parents are experts, but I asked them if they knew what it was. Right away, Dad said, "Starling, a filthy starling."

"Why does everyone hate these birds?" I asked.

"Because they are noisy and they are dirty. When I was growing up, they'd be lined up on telephone wires. People couldn't walk down the street. They're worthless."

"I think they're pretty," I said.

"In town, the police shot them as part of their job. Stratford really wanted to get rid of them."

"Why?" I asked. Dad didn't answer, because he already had.

I was surprised by his feelings. Even my brother Sandy, who is usually crazy for birds, told me over the phone that he thought starlings were junk. But I kept seeing their shiny feathers, watching how they hopped around their food, how they chased each other, how they put their long beaks deep into the ground. I would hear them buzz in the trees and think they were great.

One night, there was a nature show on TV about wildlife out west and how animals have learned to live in Vancouver. All of a sudden, there was my bird, the starling. I knew that it was here, but not there, on the edge of an ocean.

The narrator talked about how they hang around together in the afternoon and how you can't miss their roosting spots because of the noise. Then the guy said that all the starlings we've got on this continent came from about a hundred that were released in New York City in the 1890s. They'd been brought over from Europe. Didn't say why.

At the time, I guessed people must have missed them from home. But since then, I've read that some eccentric thought all of the birds mentioned by Shakespeare should live in the United States of America. Apparently, one of the Henrys has a pet starling that says, "Mortimer." Shakespeare's nightingales and skylarks didn't take, but by the middle of the twentieth century, starlings had made it to the Pacific. Now, just over a century after their first release in Central Park, there are about two hundred million.

My dad as a kid watched police shooting birds lined up in rows or gathered in roosts. This would have been in the late 1930s or so – about forty years after the first starlings were released, and already they were considered a plague. My little daddy and those cops in Stratford and a lot of others, I guess, hated something a lot like themselves. Foreign here and yet taking over everything. Messy.

A few years ago, a guy I lived with killed a starling while driving his father's station wagon. The bird had been swooping down underneath a bridge when it connected with the front roof rack and became wedged there. It hit so hard that the rack broke. All nervous and jumpy, the guy pulled over and pried the dead bird from the car. He put it down somewhere. He worried about how he was going to explain the damage to his dad.

The starling is beautiful and has much to tell. She is a shiny little fellow found all over the place, and yet I first saw her in 1990. Saw her to notice. I have no explanation for why it took me so long.

I've read that, in England, some people breed the birds to be solid white, yellow, pink, copper, grey, black, and black and white, which is called Pied. There are other specialties: Agate, Lacewing, and Isabel. These birds might sell for hundreds of pounds, and are put in shows. The starling is also a very talented mimic. Anything from a cat to a duck to a phone to a person, it can do. I've heard one that sounded like a cardinal.

I'm told that bluebirds are pretty, but I don't think I've seen any. They're harder to find. A lot of people blame starlings for that, because they're so aggressive and they take over bluebirds' nesting spots. But starlings aren't shy with people, either, while a lot of other birds are. So as we spread through Canada and the U.S., cutting down trees and putting up endless rows of awning on thousands of acres of strip malls, the starling has done well. Birds that don't like so much busy-busy, so much pavement, so many cars, so little quiet haven't done so well.

Nursing the Wound

T hings weren't going well. They were better, since she left, but they weren't good. He asked for another beer. He felt numb.

It took a couple of months before she could move out, after they'd broken up. A couple of months in a one-bedroom apartment. (She slept on the couch.) And because they knew all the same people and liked going to the same places, they'd been seeing each other all the time, even though they never talked, never told each other what plans they had. It was different since she had left. Feeling numb as he did, he didn't feel much like going to the right places or seeing anyone in particular. He just wanted to drink, but not alone.

This place was packed. People were dancing over to the right of him, some distance away from the bar. Men crowded around the edges of the dance floor. It was impossible to see who was out there. Not that he cared. The grunge on the countertop and under his nails kept him busy. He etched it carefully with the edge of a matchbook that he'd picked up here. It was more to highlight the dirt than to clean it away.

At one time, he had wanted everything with her. Even when things started to turn and they fought more often, he just figured it would happen. Some kind of permanence. Even when she said her pelvic inflammation had developed again, he hadn't let it sink in. Even when that inflammation went on for a couple of months and she didn't get it treated. Then she said she wanted to leave. She said, "I've been thinking and I decided it's over."

Not too many developers are interested in rentals when the money's in condominiums. Factories, warehouses, empty office suites, artists' lofts with artists in them: they're cleared out and converted.

He knew she had looked around. He heard that a landlord showed his ex a cramped bachelor apartment in a below-ground home reno. The owner introduced her to the throne – a toilet on a platform covered with a soiled purple shag rug. It sat ten centimetres above the rest of the floor. There was some sort of pipe running underneath. "That's why the crapper was built up so high and mighty," the owner said. Then laughed.

The apartment would have cost her nearly half her wages, after taxes. Didn't matter anyway. It was rented before she had the chance to say whether she wanted it.

So for two months, still complaining of pain, she lived with him. He worked a lot, because it was spring. People seemed to notice cracked wood and the need for decks and gazebos then. He was a carpenter. He was busy.

She was a nurse's aid, and chose to work night shifts more than before. Sometimes, though, outside of the clubs and cafés, they'd meet where they both still lived. When paths crossed within those too-close walls, she'd hold her side and complain vaguely of the eternal ache that she seemed to suffer from. Sometimes he'd imagine touching her, of soothing the ache away, but he never did.

It was his first time in this bar. The last few weeks, he'd drunk too much. He was flushed and dizzy. He turned to either side, moving his head slow to avoid feeling sick, and saw that the washrooms were down a set of stairs just behind him. He got off his stool and walked to the head of the stairs. He held the railing close, clutching with both hands, even though he knew he wasn't drunk.

Both washrooms had doors that were slightly open. The corridor between them was high and made of smooth concrete. Noises from either the Ladies or the Mens carried over to its partner. Above the row of three urinals, where the wall began to slant into the ceiling, someone had written, "Watch you fuckin head." He had to bend back a little when he went to a urinal and had a piss. Shook, tucked, zipped, then went to the sink. Washed his face; ran wet fingers through short-cropped hair.

He ran wet fingers through short-cropped hair, again and again. He felt numb and sick. Because even though he knew no one in this bar this night, he heard a familiar voice from the other washroom. A couple weeks after he'd heard that same voice repeat the ache that made her push him away, even before she said she'd leave. That made him feel obliged to carry all her stuff down the stairs when she finally did go.

"He wasn't much of a fuck," she was saying. "I mean, I know Chris was drinking and stuff – his friends told me he's liked me for a long time, you know – still, the guy wasn't great. But it's been a week since I got any. I'm hurting. Maybe I'll do better tonight." She laughed.

Leaving the bar, he was laughing. Unlocking the apartment door, he was crying. He couldn't remember the in-between. He knew he wouldn't be numb anymore. He fell asleep on the couch, too spent to notice the still-strong smell of her.

Is a Man not a Man
if a Man is a Man?

The drink in front of Carl is a local beer. There is no slice of lime or lemon on the lip of the bottle. Carl sits at the counter and talks to the bartender each time he orders. Each time, the bartender looks very bored and moves away.

The weather outside is okay, but it's late at night and cooler than usual for late spring. Carl has been in the bar for a while. He's lived in Portugal for six months. He is alone, and can speak and understand things only slowly.

Beer number four in front of Carl and a man walks into the bar, which is speckled with men and only men. But none have been worth paying much attention to. The man who just walked in is much younger than the rest. His skin has a healthy shine. He has wavy black hair and thick eyelashes. He is very cute. On the short side, well-built. There is a liveliness to him. He comes up to where Carl is sitting, orders something, gets it, then walks away. This happens quickly. Still, Carl has time to meet his eyes.

Carl drinks some of his fourth beer. The new young cute man sits by himself at a table on the other side of the room. Both men catch themselves looking at each other. Carl gives a friendly smile. The other man shifts his gaze and takes another swig of his drink.

Carl gets bored of this and decides to call it a day. He finishes the beer, says goodnight to the bartender (who doesn't answer back), and takes the path down to the beach once he gets out the door. The air bites at Carl's skin. Along the path, he sees a big rock. He sits down and looks at the stars.

A minute or two later, he hears someone else coming down the bending path. Carl sees the young man from the bar. When he reaches Carl, the man stands close and says hello in Portuguese, then unzips his pants.

Carl looks up and says his hi in a very thick accent, the inflection all wrong.

The other guy says his name, but Carl doesn't quite catch it. At the same time that he speaks, the other man pulls out his penis, stroking it a little.

Carl says, "I can speak only a little Portuguese. I understand better. What do you do?"

"I am a clown."

Carl laughs.

The cute guy says, "No, no, I *am* a clown. The circus is here now today. I am a clown in the circus." He continues to stroke himself, then says, "Are you the man or the woman?"

Carl says, "I don't think that way." He wonders what the clown looks like in makeup. The clown starts to rock his pelvis back and forth, pointing his cock to Carl's mouth. The head brushes Carl's chin every now and again.

Just for something to say, Carl says, "How long are you in town?"

"Only a few days. Want some?"

This is not the best come-on that Carl has ever heard, but he doesn't see the harm in it. He starts giving the clown head. Carl tickles the tip with his tongue, strokes the shaft firmly without squeezing too hard.

The clown says, "Put your hand there harder."

This is when they both hear thin sharp notes come through the night, bouncing along the beach. As the music gets louder, the instrument that's playing it becomes more obvious. An accordion. An accordion playing the "Skye Boat Song." While Carl is figuring out the name of the song – trying to remember it from the annual bagpipe parade in Kincardine, where his dad used to take him and his sisters and his brother and his cousins every year they spent at his grandfather's cottage – he hears the lyrics for the final verse:

> Burned are our homes, exile and death
> Scatter the loyal men
> Yet, e'er the sword cool in the sheath
> Charlie will come again.

The voice cracks a little. Just enough. Carl is swallowed up by the lilt in the voice, the lovely earnest spirit put in the words. He doesn't notice when the clown puts his penis back in his pants and zips up.

"What a surprise!" Carl calls out in English. "A bit of home, right here."

"Hallo, hallo!" says the accordion player. He speaks English with an Irish accent, or what Carl guesses is an Irish accent. Whatever it is, it is not home, but close enough.
The new man says, "Who is out here now?"

The clown's hands are in his pockets. He still stands very close to Carl, who still sits. The clown remains hopeful.

Carl says, "Over here!" It's been at least a week since he's talked with another tourist in his own language.

The accordion player isn't far away and, through the dark

gloom, comes into focus. He takes a fast glance at the two men. They are close together, but they aren't playing cards or any other obvious game. They aren't drinking. This is no fight. So why does one stand so near and the other sit? The newcomer doesn't quite know what to make of it.

"Don't mean to bother you," he says.

"No bother, we were just enjoying the beach," says Carl.

"Oh, didn't know you could see it from here. It's a bit cool. Cooler than I'd hoped."

"What brings you down here, then?" asks Carl.

"I was planning to sleep here, under the stars. Beautiful night for it, but it turns out to be too nippy for my liking. Don't have a place to sleep now, so I thought I'd pass the time with some song."

"What a drag," says Carl.

The clown, meanwhile, uses the hand in his pocket to press his cock. He has no idea what the other two are talking about. He is losing interest.

He looks steadily at Carl for a while. Carl keeps talking to the accordion player, asking where he is from and what other songs he can play.

Carl says, "You have a lovely voice."

In Portuguese, the clown finally says, "I'm going."

"Really, do you have to?"

"Yes, I work tomorrow."

This makes Carl laugh. He tells the accordion player, "He's a clown!"

"Really? Well done."

"Çiao," says the cute clown.

The accordion player pulls out some hard liquor. "This'll keep us warm, anyway," he says.

IS A MAN NOT A MAN IF A MAN IS A MAN?

The two English-speaking men from different places sit on a rock near the beach and drink. They put their arms around each other, as men do. They sing:

> Speed bonnie boat, like a bird on the wing
> Onward, the sailors cry
> Carry the lad that's born to be king
> Over the sea to Skye.

First Day

The others looked up, but said nothing. They didn't know his name, or what to say. He kept walking, nodding as he went by, moving to the desk he'd been told would be his.

When Richard sat down, he pushed his palms across the edge of the desktop. He opened all the drawers, thumbed through the paper he found there. He tested the chair a bit. Flipped the calendar beside the desk blotter to the correct date. This was his first day at a new job.

After a while, he started to get nervous. No one had come over to show him the ropes. No one had even come over to say hello, make an introduction. The people at the desks around him seemed to look at him from the corners of their eyes, with their heads bent over the papers in front of them, like they didn't want him to know they were looking at him.

Someone made a phone call, using a hissy whisper that Richard could hear. He couldn't make out the words, though.

Richard tapped a pencil against the desk pad. He looked for any manuals or binders he could read to get a head start. He fiddled with the Dilbert Day Planner. He turned on the computer. A screen message read, "Good morning user NarbeshuL." He didn't know what it meant. He remembered that, at the job interview, his boss had said there would be a two-week training period. Where was his trainer? Where was his boss? Richard tried to use the techniques he learned in stress class.

Then the boss came through a door from what Richard thought might be her office. She slowly weaved between the desks from the far end of the open-concept room. Her eyes were fixed on a space just in front of her feet as she moved. When she got near him, she had a tight, shy smile he found appealing, but she wouldn't meet his eyes. She stopped short of his desk.

"Um, what are you doing here?" she asked.

"Did I come on the wrong day? Did I get here too early?" he asked. "I'm sorry. I, I could come back. You know, I uh –"

She didn't wait for him to finish. "Um, ah, no," she said. Her name was Ruby. She'd been a manager for a couple of months now, but was still getting used to it. She was young for this position. She felt like any second now the real professionals would come and take over.

Ruby shifted her position, leaned forward a bit to get closer to the corner of the desk where the Dilbert calendar lay like an open book. She reached over and pinched the sheaf of paper with the day's date between her fingers, rubbing it.

"You changed the date," she said softly.

Richard laughed a bit. "Can't wait to get started." He looked around.

"Look, ah –"

"Richard," he said.

"Yeah, Richard. I . . . don't know how to say this, so I'm just . . . going to say it. Richard, we didn't hire you. Two days after your interview, we found someone, who'll be starting Wednesday."

"Wednesday?"

"Yes. It's Zoey. Zoey's starting. On Wednesday. She starts."

He pushed his shoulders hard into the back of the chair. He felt his muscles go soft as licorice sticks, then harden into tight bands that tied him to the chair. His breathing became short. His heart blew up against his chest. Richard thought he was going to be sick, with his head as light as it was and his body doing its own thing. He tried to put all his power into not sweating.

"I'm sorry," Ruby said. She meant it. The guy looked like he was in shock. She couldn't imagine what he was going through. It hadn't been a bad interview. She thought it would've been okay to work with him.

Finally, he looked up at her. She looked away. "But you hired me. You hired me." He almost whispered.

"No," Ruby said. "There's been some terrible mistake. I never told you you were hired. I hadn't even finished all the interviews."

"You showed me this desk. Told me I'd be working with her and her and him." He pointed around the room. The others hunched even closer to their paperwork. "You told me their names. I just can't remember. A lot of people aren't great with names. But you told me them."

"I didn't say you had the job. I talked to you about what the job would be, *if* you were hired. Who you would work with, *if* you were hired. I'm sure this has never happened before."

Richard didn't move. "You said I'd work with these people, so I thought I'd work with them."

Ruby sighed. "Well, other than saying I'm sorry again, there's not much I can do. You don't have the job. Someone else has it. She's coming in Wednesday. Her name is Zoey. There's nothing else we can do here, Richard."

Richard looked down at his palms. Black lines streaked across them. He looked at the edge of the desk. He had touched it when he first came in. Now he saw that the edge was filthy. Without thinking, he wiped his hands against his legs. He cursed under his breath when he saw that the marks had come off on his favourite mid-tone blue pants. His body pushed deeper into the chair.

Other workers coughed. Phones rang. Keyboards clicked. Sounds for new e-mail, errors, and saves. Neither of them moved.

Ruby didn't want to, but she felt she had to say something. "I can't stay here much longer. I've got work to do."

"I'm happy for you."

Ruby was losing her cool. "It would be best if you left now. I can't just leave you here."

"Fine, then," Richard said. He scanned the top of the desk. Reread the day's Dilbert. Couldn't focus on what it was about. Ties, coffee, a dog, and a manager. "Fine," he repeated. He grabbed his briefcase and pulled it on top of his lap. He sprang out of the chair and went straight through the door, keeping the briefcase high against his pants, holding it there with both hands. His elbows shot out at sharp angles. He mashed a thumb into the down button. The elevator arrived in no time, and he was gone.

When Ruby crossed the room and shut the door to her office, there was absolute silence. Then, slowly, a quiet, excited hum began to build.

Dino

Twin brothers might have been on the last bus to Brampton that night. They've been on it before. They get around. It's easy to see them. They're on the 510 Bathurst streetcar. The Flemington 100 bus. The 505 Dundas car. They're at Union Station. In Broadview Station. In Bathurst Station. They're on some bus with a final destination of Georgetown, Guelph, Brampton, Toronto. I don't remember them that night specifically, on my way back to a place between Churchville and Huttonville, but I remember them from before and after.

Bald, heavyset, matching clothes in slightly different shades. One might wear tan pants, the other fawn. Like that. With belts, but done up loose, so the waists curve around their hips and under their bellies, making the back ends baggy. Everything rumpled. They often wear thin trench coats. They almost always have rough shaves. It's hard to know how old they are. They are ancient and child-like, wrinkled and smooth.

It's true that I don't know whether these brothers were part of this particular trip I'm writing about. I'll go even further – I'll say they probably weren't. But they could have been. They should have been.

Some Toronto people like to make fun of Brampton. It was a small farm town and then a tumbled industrial city and now it's a sprawling bedroom community a bit too far away to be convenient or cool. Brampton is a little déclassé.

You can twist its name around in your mouth to make it sound foolish. Start by making a *buh* sound. Then get a tight nasal sound, hitting hard on the *r*. Sharpen the *a* to a higher pitch. Jam the *m* to the *t*. Skip the *p*. Swallow the *o*. Feel a funny buzz in the nasal area when you get to the *n*. Buhrahmt'n.

There are things not to like. There is a big boxy Costco and a House of Hair and so many strip malls it's easy to lose count. They've poured cement along the bed of creeks where people used to swim. The main roads are broad and hard and lined with trees too small to give any shade. During the day, traffic is thick and slow. But that last fact is true everywhere now. Everywhere there are too many cars.

That's not all Brampton has, though. Along these streets, people walk to temple, laughing kids ride bikes, and it's not unusual to have the bus driver strike up a conversation with you, if you're sitting at the front. A plane might come over the road, so close your body shakes. Or the sun could be just so, making all the colours in a farmer's field or on a sari shimmer right into you.

In the late fall, you might ride a bike along Steeles Avenue. Passing transport trucks create a vacuum that is hard to fight, but you have to or else you'll be pulled into the road. To your right, there is a square cluster of trees, with a huge swath of cut corn stalks around it. Above – massive electrical pylons and power lines. Despite the wind and the grit and your fear of traffic – despite the noise from automobiles, trucks, and planes – you can hear the dense clacking of the roost of starlings hidden in those trees.

The twins have this kind of beauty. I remember seeing them on a southbound 510 Bathurst streetcar, on its way to the Canadian National Exhibition grounds. One brother sat behind the other on the single seats on the driver's side. They sat with their shoulders sloped. Their heads slowly bobbed to the left, to see what was going on outside the window they leaned against. Then one brother bent forward to get closer to the other. He brought his right arm up, with his pointer finger out. He looked at the back of his brother's head, and gradually pushed his finger into the brother's back. Then he poked again, and again, with a gap between each effort. The brother being poked didn't stir. Still, the poking continued. The expressions on both brothers' faces didn't change.

In a way, all of this is Dino: the brothers, the birds, the streets, and the city of Brampton.

It was 11:40 PM and the last bus going to Brampton started its route. I looked out to see things filtered by tinted glass and the night. The people outside had that uncomfortable edge of happiness brought on by summer holidays. When we got going, lights along the road sometimes made things brighter, but sometimes they weren't around. The bus pulled over a lot. It went into the airport and picked up people working late there, then went through a couple of high-end subdivisions, where nobody got on or off. We went along Steeles, and passed the small lot of densely packed trees roiling with starlings. I couldn't hear them. The bus wound into the centre of Brampton, where it stopped at city hall's garden before going on to the station, where everyone who was left got out.

There weren't many people around. I walked along the platform and through an archway, out to Nelson Street. I sat on an empty bench in front of the station, and waited for my friend and neighbour, Michael, who was coming to pick me up. In no time, I saw his grey Volvo station wagon come down the street and slowly, slowly pass me by. I waved, but saw that the driver was preoccupied. At the stop sign just east of me, he made a left turn and disappeared. I figured that I must have made a mistake. I was sure it had been Michael's car with Michael in it, but then why didn't he stop? And why didn't he come back? I waited.

It was a cool August night. I wasn't dressed for waiting. On the west end of the station, a few taxi cabs were ready for customers who likely would not come. The cabbies talked to each other. I sat on the bench alone, watching an occasional car go by.

Three guys came from the direction where the phantom Michael had disappeared. The guys were joking loudly with each other, one saying "Nah, nah." Another saying, "You did!" The third was clapping his hands and laughing. I heard this more than saw it. I was worried about getting involved. They walked behind me. I noticed from the corner of my eye that they threw themselves onto a bench further along from mine. After a while, one of them got up and wobbled over to me. He looked at me, smiled, and asked, "What are you doing here?"

It was close to one in the morning.

"I'm waiting for a friend," I said.

"But what are you doing here, waiting for somebody?"

"He's supposed to pick me up."

"Who is he?"

"Michael. His name is Michael."

"Your boyfriend?"

"No, just a friend. He's married, has kids. We live in the same area."

"Can I sit down?"

I said, "Sure. I wouldn't mind the company while I wait."

"What do you mean?" he said.

"Well, I'm sitting here by myself."

"Oh, yeah. Do you want some pizza?" He had a slim kraft paper bag jacketing two slices on a cardboard triangle.

"No thanks."

"You sure?"

"Yeah, thanks."

"Okay. My name is Dino." He was short, like me. A wiry, bird-like man. Thin-boned. Ready to fly. He wore blue jeans, a guyish jacket, and a baseball cap right-way around. His sandy hair fell across his forehead, over his ears and down his neck a bit. His face was somehow both chalk white and a solid deep red. He smoked. I thought about when he'd have his first heart attack.

We shook hands.

"You sure you don't want a piece? It's nice and hot. I just got it." He pulled a slice out of the bag. It was big, covered in pepperoni, cheese, and tomato sauce.

I said, "Actually, I just came in from Toronto. Some friends had people over for dinner. I'm full, thanks."

Dino said, "You don't look full."

I was ninety pounds and broken hearted. I didn't have much of an appetite.

As the conversation went on, it was mostly pleasant. Dino got angry at one point. He thought I was claiming my father owned a building across the street. But we cleared that up. I had been answering his question about where I lived, which was not across the street. The old brick office block just got in the way of the direction where I was pointing. Way down there, over to the right.

"Oh, east, you mean."

"No, it's west."

"No. It's south and east of here. That's where you live. Where is it that you live?" He was getting upset again. I asked him what he was up to that night.

By now he was well into his second slice of pizza. He had told me how snobby the people in Georgetown were. He was convinced I came from there, even though he also thought I was nice. Dino said, "It really looks to me like you could use some of my pizza. Get some meat on you. I'm almost done here, but there's still the crust. You could have my crust. It would be like our first date."

I said no thanks again, and that I wasn't hungry. It wasn't completely true; I was getting hungry, out in the cold, waiting for Michael to come pick me up. But I'm a vegetarian, so there was no chance of my being tempted by that pepperoni pizza slice, even if the only thing left was the crust.

I got off the bench and looked up and down the street for any sign of Michael.

"Forty more pounds and you'd be perfect," Dino said. "Even now, you have a nice ass. Those pants are nice on you."

When I looked at him, Dino said, "No, I mean it. They're different. I have a pair of pants that are kind of purple. Jeans, but with a different kind of cut. I know they look really good. I like those pants, too."

"They sound like a nice pair of pants," I said.

"What?"

"I bet they're good-looking pants."

"Yeah. I went into a bar once, and this guy said, 'Hey, nice pair of pants.' I asked him, 'What do you mean by that?' I was getting ready for a fight. But he just said, 'I mean I really like your pants.' And he did. They are nice pants. So are yours."

"Thanks."

Dino asked, "Are you cold?"

My arms were crossed tight in front of me. I might have been shivering a little. Still, I said no.

"You gotta be cold. You're so little."

I kept looking up and down the street. I was pacing a little. Dino said, "Yeah, all you really need is forty pounds. And you already have a pretty good ass."

I looked over to the taxi stand and saw two cars idling there. I told Dino I had to go.

"I know, I'm bugging you," he said.

"No, I really appreciated the company, Dino."

"What do you mean by that?"

I said, "I mean I couldn't think of a better way to pass the time. You were good company. But I have to go now. It's getting late."

In a quiet way, Dino said, "That's the nicest thing anyone has ever said to me. It really is."

As I walked to the taxis, he shouted behind me, "Forty pounds! You can do it! I know you can!" I looked back at him. His thumbs were both up. He laughed.

Award Winning

Three hundred people in a room with high ceilings. Three hundred people, worrying about threads, runs in pantyhose, a spill on silk. Three hundred people drinking too much in an ornate, airy, white waiting room. The bartenders, with their black bow-ties, refuse to make eye contact. It is time to celebrate and acknowledge the accomplishments of those nominated today. There will only be one official winner, but remember that all nominees are winners. The judges and all those attending this event admire each person whose contribution is being considered for this honour. The award's recipient will be announced after the meal. Enjoy.

Manjula Rao walks past the people crowded but not touching at the bar. She is a stranger to most of them, but nods to the few she knows. Some don't nod back. She takes off her winter coat. She walks over to the next room, where outerwear is being checked. There is a small lineup, but a few people stand chatting with each after they drop things off, blocking the way for others. It takes longer than it should for Manjula to hand over her long purple crushed-velvet coat and get a paper number that will allow her to get the coat back.

When she returns to the waiting room, Manjula sees that people have started to go into the Bonaventure Ballroom. She sees her friend, Amy Morse, at the front of the crowd. They are supposed to sit together. Amy doesn't see her friend, and goes in without her.

Manjula passes the bar and the display table with her picture on it. By the time she gets to the ballroom doors, there aren't too many people waiting to get in. She can now see that there is a big deal with tickets. But she hadn't been told that she needed a ticket, and no one gave her a ticket, and she had called the organizers a couple of times to make sure everything was arranged. Manjula thinks that, as a nominee, she might not need one. She is now at the front of the line.

A squat, surly fellow in a tuxedo says, "Can I have your ticket." It isn't a question.

"I'm one of the nominees," she says. "I don't have a ticket."

"Over there," he says. The man jerks his head at a series of tables lined up in a tight row. He looks at the torn tickets in his hands.

She goes. She asks for a ticket. The new man says, "No, you have to go over there," and points further down the row. She goes. Here sit three women with legs crossed at their calves. Volunteers. All of them clearly had their hair professionally done this very morning. Crisp curls. Colour so flawlessly bland it almost looks natural. These women are deep in conversation with a couple of other attendees. Manjula waits a few minutes while the two people at her side struggle to figure out their own ticket issues. The couple and the seated ladies all have furrowed brows. Because she is preoccupied by the time passing, Manjula finds it hard to follow the conversation. All involved are picking up envelopes, looking at the stiff slips inside. Meanwhile, the waiting room is emptying out. The ballroom is filling up. Finally, the couple goes away, envelope and enclosed tickets in hand. One of the wonderfully concerned volunteers looks up to Manjula and asks how she can be of assistance.

"I'm one of the nominees. I can't get in without a ticket. No one told me about a ticket."

"What is your name, dear?"

"Manjula Rao."

"And who are you with?"

"No one, really. I'm one of the nominees."

"Really. And you are, again?"

During this conversation, the middle woman puts on half-glasses. She pulls a list from a file folder. She finds a ruler and a pen. Her eyes run down hand-written names on a grid, pen poised to neatly strike out the appropriate line using the ruler. The third woman plucks nervously at the modest hem of her dress.

One of the judges approaches the table. Manjula doesn't recognize him as a judge until he says, "I'm Philip Edgars. I am one of the judges." The third woman looks up from her skirt, smiles, and hands him a ticket. He leaves for the Bonaventure Ballroom. During his wait, Philip Edgars had ignored Manjula completely.

She is becoming impatient. "Look, my picture is right over there, on the nominees' table. Right over there," she says. "Manjula Rao. I'm one of the nominees. Take a look. You will recognize me. I still look pretty much the same. I've changed my hair a little, but I think you'll see."

The first volunteer asks, "Did you speak with David Smith?"

"I don't know anyone. I was nominated. I'm not good with names. I'm supposed to sit with my friend, Amy Morse. She's sitting with other people she knows. I only know her, really. And not that well."

The woman says, "Oh, you'll sit at an open table. Nominees don't get to choose where they sit. Unless someone else gets them a ticket. Unless someone else arranges to sit with them."

"What? But I was told I could. I phoned the office weeks ago to make sure I could sit with Amy." Manjula can feel the sweat build under her arms. She does not want to spoil her look. She will try to remember not to lift her arms too high during and after lunch. She is trying to stop tears from pooling in her eyes.

"Oh, I see. Well, we have no record of this arrangement." The volunteer who's talking looks to the volunteer in glasses. Still going over the list, the latter shakes her head. The talking volunteer glares at Manjula, then says, "We have no record of you. Maybe your ticket is in the envelope for your friend's table. Maybe they have your ticket and didn't tell me. Just a minute, I'll go see."

The volunteer uncrosses her legs. She pops up from her chair and disappears into the Bonaventure Ballroom. Manjula waits by the table. She looks around the white waiting room. Other than the three volunteers behind the plywood tables covered in fine white linens, there are few people left. The nominee can tell that these people have been looking at her, but now that she is looking at them, their heads are tilted away. She wonders how high the ceiling is, what exact colour the floor would be called. Her eyes drift to the display where all the nominees' 8x10 glossy photos have been mounted. There she is. She looks at the two remaining lady volunteers, but they are busy with something.

It seems like the woman who ran into the Bonaventure Ballroom will never come back. Manjula wonders what is happening. She doesn't know that Amy Morse is in the washroom freshening up before the meal. And that the volunteer has found Amy Morse's table, and is asking strangers whether they have the nominee's ticket. The people at the table say, "Angela? I'm sorry, I don't know her. She's nominated? She's sitting at our table? We don't have an envelope." They want lunch to be served soon, so they can get back to work.

In the waiting room, Manjula starts to feel silly about standing at the ticket table for so long. She is reminded of grade one, when the teacher did all sorts of crushing little things that made her feel different in a terrible way. In a way Manjula could not change. Now a grown woman, she tries not to feel so doomed. She tries to keep herself from walking out. She thinks about how this nomination is good for her. She thinks about grace.

She thinks about a chained little monkey in a bellhop's suit, dancing on top of an organ-grinder's instrument, holding out a cup. If the performers succeed, they can have dinner. In exchange, people with extra money can be entertained.

She thinks about making her parents proud. She thinks about how her relationship needs some work. She reminds herself that she is partly here for those who believe in her, and partly here for other people who really should be here but aren't. She doesn't want to do something that will make them all look bad. She thinks about an earlier relationship that went sour years before. That person should have been nicer to her.

Manjula steps away from the ticket table and leans against a carved pillar. She looks through the open doors into the Bonaventure Ballroom with what she hopes will pass as sophistication and detachment.

She sees Amy sit back down at table 123. Her friend is laughing, touching someone's arm. At one point, Amy looks over to the entryway. She is frowning. When she sees Manjula there, she stands up. She waves her arms. She smiles and points to the table, mouthing, "Over here." Manjula shrugs. She raises her hands, palms up, to show she is helpless. Amy doesn't understand.

Manjula says quietly, "I can't come in. They won't let me in." Amy is laughing now, shaking her head that she can't understand. Manjula raises her voice, "I can't come in." She shakes her head and points to the table, pouting. Amy shrugs. As loudly as she dares, Manjula says, "I can't come in. They won't let me in." Manjula wants Amy to hear, way over there through the doors and into the centre of the Bonaventure Ballroom. But Amy can't hear, so she sits back down and starts talking with yet another person at table 123.

The ticket taker still stands at the doors. He is having grumpy daydreams and doesn't notice the friends. It's not his problem.

Finally, the volunteer who is getting to the bottom of things comes back. She says, "Okay, I'm going to have to give you a ticket." She pulls some tickets from her pocket and looks at them. With her other hand, she slides the top ticket off and begins to pass it to Manjula. It is just within grasp when she pulls it back. "Oh wait, I have to write your name on it. It's, it's Angela –"

The nominee sighs loudly. "My name is Manjula Rao." She spells it out.

Manjula Rao, the well-bred woman writes across the top of the ticket, in a very pretty, slow script. She gives it to Manjula with a tight polite smile, then says, "Yes, you'll be sitting at table 134."

Manjula smiles back. "I'll be sitting with Amy Morse," she says. She walks to the big carved-mahogany doors yawning from the ballroom.

Manjula hands her ticket to the surly man. The surly man starts to tear it, even while Manjula's fingers grip the edge. Another pleasant volunteer suddenly emerges from the bowels of the Bonaventure Ballroom. She wears very sensible formal shoes and is much shorter than Manjula. She touches the ticket and the hands holding it, stopping the ripping ritual cold. She says she is here to direct Angela to where she will sit. Manjula says, "That's okay, I'm sitting over there." She points over to table 123, where there are two empty chairs several seats away from Amy Morse.

The latest respectable lady's face goes a bit spongy. Her lips thin. She shakes her head. She says, "No, no," in a sharp disapproving tone that some older people can get away with, and points her free hand in another direction. She turns her face there too. The volunteer's other hand – now cupped over the ticket – will soon be tightly clamped on Manjula. The volunteer will guide the nominee to her proper place.

While she still has a chance, Manjula lets go of her half of the partially torn ticket and, in surprise, so does the surly ticket taker. It feathers down to the marble floor. In slippery white satin shoes and a short skirt she bought used two years ago, Manjula roughly shoulders past this latest table-seating woman. The nominee is worried that she might knock the delicate creature over, but panic takes hold. She bolts to the table where she now needs to sit, has to sit. Her eighty-dollar blouse is new.

She sits down in one of the two empty chairs at table 123. She is full of a light nervous laughter that makes the others at the table look her way. Amy Morse says hello, and asks what took her so long. Manjula begins to talk in a breathless, high voice about what just happened. She laughs between each sentence.

As she is telling the story, another pleasant looking woman comes from behind and says, "Are you Manjula Rao?" When Manjula turns to see who is speaking, this woman says, "I'm so sorry –"

Manjula cuts her off, saying, "Look, I don't want to talk about it now." The woman goes away, troubled. Manjula picks up where she left off, dominating all conversation at the table where she knows one person. Manjula is in good spirits – giddy, almost. Drunk on humiliation.

A group of flushed white people enters the Bonaventure Ballroom. A collared minister dressed in traditional black heads the line. At the end of the clump is the renowned and respected main speaker – a leading light in the field – some distance from the rest. With their arrival, a flustered woman runs into the room. She asks a volunteer where she can sit, saying that she is one of the judges. This volunteer places the newcomer in the one remaining chair at table 123. Beside nominee Manjula Rao.

The judge looks around and says, "I lost track of the time. I was at the pre-luncheon cocktails. . . . No one thought to tell me the lunch was about to begin." She introduces herself properly. The others at the table say who they are. When it is Manjula's turn, she says her name, then adds, "I'm one of the nominees."

"You do fine work," the judge says, but doesn't have the heart to look directly at her. "Fine work."

The minister blesses the beautiful accomplishments of those being considered for the award. The people in the room are asked to stand for a toast to their country. When everyone is seated again, the MC notes the presence of high school students from around the city. The teenagers are asked to stand and be acknowledged with applause. The people at the head table are named, their companies and titles mentioned. Lunch is eaten. The famous keynote speaker speaks. The winner is announced. Then everyone goes back to what they need to do.

Red

The barbecue is the splatter and smell. Waves of dry heat edged with animal fat. Warmed by the kind of friendships that last forever. The friendships laced with jealousy and fear, underlined by a strange kind of mutual loathing and need. Some might say best friends.

They speak of small things. Movies. Sports. Work. Celebrities. Hair, clothes, and weight. Growing old. They talk about other people who aren't here, around the spittle of the grill. These others just aren't quite right, somehow. Not as good. Not at the barbecue. Not invited.

The host's girlfriend has gone on some kind of business trip. She's been gone for quite a while. She phones once a week or so. She gets things done.

⋘◉⋗◉⋙

There's already been a bit of an argument. The host is a bit upset that Arrow doesn't want to see *JFK*. The host, Greg, is Arrow's boyfriend's best friend.

When he questioned her about it, Arrow had said, "But I don't like Oliver Stone. His characters stink."

"Come on!" Greg said. "What about the editing? You can't cut yourself off like that, Arrow!"

She said, "I think I'll have a full life despite this decision."

He hates her sarcasm.

Arrow has heard very unappealing things about Greg from her boyfriend, Chris, who isn't sitting with her right now. Her boyfriend walked away from conversation, keeping himself busy with things he has never noticed before, things that take him away from talking to his buddy and his girlfriend. Plants, grass, and flowers.

She is bored with talking about movies she hasn't seen and doesn't want to see and people she doesn't really know or care about. Arrow asks, "Greg, what have you been up to?"

The host says, "I know it repulses you, but I couldn't live without it. Couldn't live without it. Don't even want to try."

Arrow doesn't follow. She asks, "Pardon?"

He says, "I know what you are thinking. I go to a religious butcher. They know what they are doing."

She still doesn't understand. "I'm sorry –"

The grass is dry. There is this frail stinking wet that clings to the air – it clings to everything. Crickets and other bugs. Some flies. The sun sucking brains out of heads.

Greg interrupts her. He says, "We got vegetables for you. But I couldn't live that way. Just couldn't."

He asks, "Have you had my tomato salad? I make a good one. Give you the recipe. But I need more to be satisfied. I need a little meat, every day."

Arrow hadn't said anything about the blood thickening on the plate of raw steak, pooling over the delicate yellow daisy chain laced with gold detailed on bone white. She doesn't know why Greg is stuck on this track.

She says, "I was just asking what –"

"Ya, I guess the look must turn your gut. What can I say? I'm sorry, I don't want to apologize. I don't like all this holier-than-thou. There are unhappy people trying to do the right thing being all holier-than-thou because they are so miserable. Who needs it?"

Arrow sits at the picnic table. Her boyfriend has abandoned her, looking carefully at plants he knows nothing about. He knows nothing about plants, and thinks about how lonely he is, always.

Arrow asks, "What about that Brenda Houseman, anyway?"

Greg smiles. "Oh, I didn't know you knew her. What'd she do now?"

boygirlhappy

The three adults at the table don't hear the children arguing beside them. Instead, they talk about grown-up things.

The children's aunt finishes up in the basement bathroom. She comes up the stairs. The children, Alice and Billy, are standing at the head of these stairs. The aunt, Elaine, hears them before she sees them.

"You're a girl."

"No, I'm not."

"You're a girl."

"No, I'm not."

"You're a girl."

"No, I'm not." By this time, her nephew's voice is quavering, unsure.

Aunt Elaine gets to the top of the stairs. She says, "Number one: Alice, you are a girl, so I don't understand why you would call someone a girl as an insult. Number two: Billy, you are obviously not a girl, so anyone calling you that is just being silly. Also, it's fine to be a girl, so I don't understand why you are so upset."

The kids jab their feet into the parquet floor. They keep their eyes down. Their mouths are slack. They don't say anything. The adults at the table don't notice this other conversation. They keep talking about world affairs. *Are we strong enough to go the distance? We must give up some freedoms to save Freedom. A firm hand.*

You're a girl, you're a girl, you're a girl, you're a girl. She could never say, "No, I'm not."

Elaine has three brothers. Growing up, the boys reminded her that she was different every chance they got. Elaine was the middle child, but her brothers made sure she felt like the last.

See this picture? You gotta get boobies like this and a butt like this if you want to be a lady.

Look at her! She's flat as a board!

Girls can't do that.

You can't come. You're a girl.

She made up a boy's checklist when she was twelve and really mad:

- Melt plastic soldiers with a match.
- Put wax crayons on the old radiator.
- Hold a magnifying glass to bugs that scurry from the heat, then become puffs of smoke.
- Get a bucket of frogs' eggs and let it dry out in the sun.
- Burn hair.
- Pull everything apart and watch what leaks out.
- Cut, scrape, pick, hit, race, break, fight, scream, order, taunt.
- Blame others for your troubles.
- Be little kings of the world.
- Be mad because you should be a king, but aren't.

Elaine is biased. The smell of boyhood haunts her. She hated boys. She wanted to beat the shit out of all the ones who were bullies, but felt sorry for the bullies, too. She loved boys. She wanted to smooth worries away from angry ones. She wanted to be a boy so bad she dreamed about it.

She wanted to be unable to imagine what it is to be a girl.

Sometimes, she still wants this.

"What is your point?" Chris says. Elaine has been going on for quite some time, and he's getting bored and confused.

Elaine says, "I don't know what you mean. I was just telling you something."

"But what is the point? Why are you telling me?"

She says, "I just thought you might be interested."

Chris says, "Interested in what? I don't have a clue what the story is. I don't know what the point is."

"Okay," she says, "I wasn't thinking about a point. I was just saying what happened. Forget it."

"Why are chicks so vague?" Chris says. "Round and round and round, going nowhere."

Elaine says, "I'm going home."

Chris looks at her, disgusted. "What's wrong now? You lose an argument and pull out a pout. Don't start crying. Christ, I can't stand it when girls cry over nothing."

"I'm going home," she says again.

"Fine," he says. "Be a baby. You'll tell me why you're so upset when you get around to it, I'm sure."

She thinks about asking him if he really doesn't understand what's wrong. She doesn't ask. She knows he really doesn't, which makes her feel worse. She finds it hard to believe, but she knows, she knows. And having the words come out of him, aimed at her, would be more than she could take.

Hearing him say, "No, no I don't." Hearing him say, "What am I, a mind reader?" Hearing him say, "Maybe if you gave me a hint, a clue, I could play this stupid game." Hearing it from his mouth, in his voice, travelling the air, crashing against her ear, and slicing into her brain. It would be too much.

Better to have it known yet unsaid, leaving room for the hope that she could be wrong.

A few days later, Elaine breaks up with Chris.

Boy Crazy
Tomboy
Boyish
Boyfriend
Old Boys
Girlish
Girlie
Girly
Girlfriend
Old Girl

Elaine has no children. She doesn't want a girl or a boy. She doesn't want to see the pressure and the panic in her own child's eyes. She wants boygirlhappy before anyone else is born. She wants to be who she is, whatever that means. A time when people can be a boy in a girl's body or a girl in a boy's body or a girly girl or a boyish girl or something else, something entirely new and hard to imagine, us in our isolation cells of gender. She longs for a time when everyone could love how and whom they please without fear. When everyone could love.

Her relationships never seem to last more than a couple of

years. Her parents tell her she takes her work too seriously. Her closest girl cousin tells her she should choose men with more drive. A friend says she has too much ambition, and that it gets in the way of commitment and turns off too many men.

Her brothers don't talk to her much about anything other than their work. She doesn't see them often, anyway, what with their families, jobs, and homes.

After the break-up, Chris follows her in his car for a few weeks. He phones. He pops over for visits because he "happens to be in the area." He hides love notes around the place when he comes around. He says he's been thinking about everything, and he's really sorry. He's learned his lesson. He starts to call her parents Mom and Dad.

Elaine tells him she is less lonely now.

Chris cries. "I take it back," he says. "I take it all back."

"There's no going back," Elaine says. "We're stuck here."

Elaine is at a party. Chris's best friend comes over to say hello. He tells her a bit about his own relationship. It has ups and downs. "I told Becky not to even think about leaving. I told her I'll seduce her closest friends," he says. "I know I'm not the best-looking guy, but I have a certain charm. I could do it. I could sleep with them, I'm almost sure. Well, most, if not all, anyway."

Elaine doesn't know how to respond. She says, "Nice party."

"Yeah, it's awful," he says. "But it's true. I will."

A couple of years later, Elaine has managed to shift her circle. She doesn't see much of Chris and his friends, which is a relief. But one night, she sees her ex at a table with a bunch of people she doesn't recognize. A few of them keep looking over at her, then looking away when she meets their eyes. She gets as depressed as she's ever been. She decides she basically hates Chris. Then she feels much better.

The next day, she phones someone she basically likes. They decide to go dancing, but neither knows if this is really a date, or if they're hanging out as friends. Before this, they've only seen each other dancing with other people at a gay bar. Neither knows if the other is even interested. They just know they both love to dance.

The night they go out, they jump around and swing their arms all crazy. They bump into each other. They start kissing while retro-eighties music plays. It's a date.

Doug is a girlish boy; Elaine is a boyish girl. For the first time, things fit. They are boygirlhappy together.

Elaine's nephew and niece, Billy and Alice, live with their parents in the suburbs. The streets twist around. There are lots of dead-ends and crescents in the neighbourhood. The houses come in three models and are all about twenty-five years old. Most people paint things in neutral tones, but every once in a while there is a pink garage door or burnt-orange trim with purple detailing. A couple of houses try to pass as Victorian, with ornate gingerbread trim that someone cut out of plywood using a jigsaw in a handyman's workshop.

When Billy was a baby, his grandparents would take him in a stroller to the mall nearby. When he was old enough to walk, Billy would still go in the stroller because it was such a big trip. But when they were coming back, he would make a fuss a block away from home. His grandparents would let him out. Billy would walk to the stop sign at the corner of his street. He would bend down and touch the ground around the sign. Then Billy would walk up to the sign and hug it. Then he'd take his grandparent's hands and walk the rest of the way.

When Alice was a baby, she needed order and routine. If there were a lot of people over, and they started to hive off into different rooms, Alice would go into the kitchen and take a grown-up by the hand. She would bring the person to the living room and point to a chair. Her face was very serious. She would back up into her own little rocker, and watch for any movement. If the grown-up stayed still, she got up to find someone else.

Alice would go through the house and bring everyone to the living room, one by one. If anyone tried to leave, Alice would jump up and push hard on thighs until the person sat back down. She would walk backwards, never looking over her shoulder to see where she was going. Her chubby hands feeling behind her for the little rocker. When she found it, Alice would sit down and keep her eyes on the people in the room.

Billy and Alice's mother says she would never take her kids to the Pride Day parade. "It's confusing enough," she says, "I don't want to make things harder than they have to be." Elaine disagrees but keeps quiet. Boys learn to be boys. Girls learn to be girls. Life is so much stupid misery.

That night, out on a date, Doug says, "I want to be your housewife." Elaine laughs and hugs him tight.

Cockroach

She wakes up, her hard shell aching. She wakes up, and her shell is not a shell anymore. She sees brightness. She is not where she belongs. She is outside and on her back. Her guts are somehow exposed, she can feel it. This is dangerous.

"Cat still got your tongue?" It talks to her differently than she's heard from them before. And she understands. She thinks of the touch of antennae before mating. She thinks of the failing love song of a desperate male. This sound comes from a creature she would once have run from, but there is no way to scuttle: she is damaged. She sees it stand on two legs. Before, she knew only hands and feet, quaking floors, and massive shadows.

Everything is smaller. She's been here before in this alley, but things look different from what she knows. Exotic yet familiar. Like déjà vu. It all looks flat and finite, but busier. So many details lost. The light is not the light she knows. There is this *colour*. She finds it hard to focus. Her head hurts.

"Been lying here three days, saying nothing, doing nothing. I'm not gonna bite."

She looks at its feet.

It asks, "What's your name?"

She knows she has to make sound back. She is stuck here, and must fit in or be destroyed. She has seen the heel come down on others. She says what she's heard most from the creatures. She croaks, "Roach." But this is her first time, and her voice is weak. It cracks and gasps.

"Roshe? That's unusual. Where you from?"

She moves her head, sees only strangeness nearby. It starts to sink in that the strangeness is a squishy bloated version of the body she once had, missing whole parts. She brings her front leg to the top of her head, wanting to touch an antenna. Nothing but limp strands that cannot sense. She sees no middle legs. She is so huge. She will never fit small gaps again. She is one of them. A creature. Nightmares are very new to her.

She cries. Her head feels strange with the wet, but the moistness is a comfort, too. She curls tighter on the dirty mattress by the fire escape.

On the other side of the alley, she sees a bug's hard brown shell shine on dull bricks in the early morning light. She knows it's time to find the cool dark safe place. The bug has the form to get there; so small, so far from her. She would like to touch antennae, do some posturing, get acquainted, then quickly move along. But if she moved, with this alien form, the cockroach would just disappear. It doesn't matter: it's already gone.

"I love you," she pleads. "Please take me back. What did I do wrong?"

The big thing laughs, leans against the alley wall. "You love me? You want me back?"

"No. To see things right again. To be a part of things."

There is quiet for a while.

"What do you do, like this?" She moves a front leg around her puffy body, stripped of protection. She tries to get more of a sense of things from her lower end, but there are no signals. Warnings have been cut off. She is so frightened.

"What do you mean?"

"What is it to be like this?"

"Like what?"

"Like one of you."

"Like me? Like a guy?"

"Like one of you," she says. "Like any one of you. Not the cluster, but the one."

"Well, where have you been?"

She says, "It's all murky."

It looks thoughtful, then says, "It depends. It's all –"

"I want to go back," she cries. "I want to go back."

"You must have left for a reason."

"I didn't leave. Why am I here like this?"

It says, "Isn't that one of life's great mysteries?"

Caddish

Hair light brown with kinky white strands standing out thick at odd angles, cut in blunt chunks. Triangled at the back. He did the job himself. "I just don't trust barbers," he would say, if anyone asked, and sometimes even when no one did. "Sixteen bucks for what?"

He was seriously thinning up top in a monkish manner. He had food on a front tooth. David was in the regular restaurant. He was wearing flannel pants, just a little high on his ankles, tight around a thickening waist. Light grey socks. He was slouched back in a padded green leatherette chair with chrome legs and frame. He held a cigarette high in his left hand. The restaurant hummed and crackled with the sound of the smoke eater above the table. The radio behind the counter was on low. Some ash drifted down the front of David's drab shirt, but he didn't see it. He was poking at what was left of his bacon and eggs. He was making a pitch.

"Why not? Why not a health food store?" David said.

Across from him sat his unhappy brother, who was much younger. Still, this made him a man in his late thirties. He also cut his own hair, but for different reasons, which he would not discuss. He thought he did a better job than his older brother did. Freddie looked at the long scraggly hairs riding on the dome of David's head with a mixture of horror and revulsion. Without thinking, he touched his own crown.

Sitting in the restaurant, Freddie wished David would stop playing with the cold, congealed meal in front of him. He didn't like to see fat mixing with the runny egg. He didn't want to see the white toast soften into a pulp. The raspberry jam smeared on the side of the plate made Freddie uneasy.

"Why a health food business? What's it to you?"

"It's good business, a growing industry. You know. You're a vegetarian now, right? All the good it does you."

"That's my own business. Which, by the way, isn't the same as running a store," said Freddie. He was unhappy because he basically didn't like his family. He couldn't admit that to himself, though. So, to keep off the scent of discontent, the guy made an effort to have weekly brunches at the regular restaurant with his older brother, and sulky family dinners every Thursday with his parents and sister.

David, on the other hand, hardly ever saw the rest of the family. One of his favourite weekly topics when the two brothers got together was how and why he hated each family member, present company excepted. He also liked explaining his theories about why he wasn't obliged to pay back all the money his mother insisted on calling loans. And exploring why she kept giving him more. "She only does it so she can see me," he'd say. "She knows without the money I'd never come around. So why not? We both get what we want. Why she wants it, don't ask me."

David basically didn't like Freddie, either, but he liked to see his little brother squirm. Also, if Freddie could snap out of being scared shitless and depressed because the world revolved without his permission, he would probably have a good head on his shoulders. Good for business, and useful to the older brother.

"You want more coffee?" asked the waiter, who was also the cook. He had come up to them, quiet as a thief. The younger brother wondered when the man's apron was last washed. The younger brother already felt nervous and slightly sick. He shook his head no, looking at the table.

"Sure, sure. Thanks," said David, laughing and making a big show of lifting his cup up for more. After the waiter left, David said, "Their coffee really stinks. Always has. You think they just keep the same pot, adding more water as it gets low, heating it up again in the morning?"

"So why drink it?"

"Why not? What else should I do?" The older brother shifted around in his chair. He put his right ankle on his left knee. Freddie could see David's fishy pale skin between his frayed pant cuff and the top of his sock. He could see that his brother's dark leg hairs were disappearing with age. He wondered what David spent their mother's money on. Freddie thought about how he might be stuck supporting his parents down the road, and how there might be nothing to inherit, thanks to David and their sister. He coughed when he swallowed his water wrong.

David said, "See? Anything can get you. So why be a worry wart all the time? Why not have fun?"

"Is that what you're going to tell your customers?"

"What customers?"

"The ones at this health food store."

"Oh, you're going to deal with the customers. I'm the man behind the scenes."

"I couldn't handle the customers."

"You've got a natural talent. Good with figures. Guilty about everything. And such a worrier. You'll get everybody hooked on the pills and supplements and . . . what are they, tinctures?"

"They're called tinctures, yes." Freddie was sure he was getting a cold.

"Anyway, what a racket."

"Could we talk about something else?"

"I'm serious."

"Well, so am I," said Freddie. "Could we talk about something else?"

"We've already done family. What else is there?"

"Ah, what's new with you?"

David answered, "What do you mean?"

"Just that. What's been happening lately?"

"I'm doing fine. Fine. As well as you. Maybe better. I might not have some sort of fancy office job, but there's a lot going on out there. A lot is happening. You've got to take risks though, Freddie. You've got to take risks to get anywhere these days." Then he said, "Have you played the new PlayStation? It's great. I was over at Stephanie's place. Her kid just got it. He's good, too."

"When was the last time you visited Mom and Dad?"

"We already did family."

"Come on, when?"

A fly in the water glass. A hockey report turned up louder on the radio. The sun shifting down a bit so the whole place flooded with light. Dust everywhere. Finally, David said, "Last week."

Freddie put his hands on the table and looked at them. "Right," he said.

"'Right. Right,'" said David. "What 'Right'? What right you got Mr High-and-Mighty? Mr My-Shit-Don't-Stink? Mr Son-Who-Can-Do-No-Wrong? Mr I-Feel-Sick?"

"Okay, can we change the subject? Can we really change the subject?" With the sunlight now blasting through the big panel windows at the front, Freddie saw all the spots on the dishes and the glasses and the silverware that the guy who washed had missed. As if the fly in the glass wasn't bad enough. He felt so bad, but Freddie didn't have the heart to do anything for the fly. He was afraid David would make fun of him if he tried a rescue. So the fly circled the glass on its back, floating on the water, round and round. Freddie had never been in the restaurant so late. He was sorry to be there at all, but especially at a time of day when he could see so much.

David picked up the newspaper crossword puzzle he had been working on earlier. He filled in a few more boxes with letters. He looked at some of the sports scores. He muttered, "What's with him, anyway? Is he their accountant? Their avenging angel? The hand of justice? From the day of his birth, I've wondered the same things. From his crib he's been an *alter kaker*."

Freddie said, "I heard that. Don't need to take it from you. No sir. No more." He stood up, put on his coat and snatched the bill from its plate. "I'll get this," he said, "I'll pay it with my own money, that I earned."

David didn't look up from the paper. He said, "Well, lah-dee-dah and whoop-dee-do." As Freddie walked away, David shouted, "Till next week, little one!"

The fly buzzed in the glass.

Outside, Freddie thought about when he was small. He thought about his brother and sister, about his mom and dad. He wondered how people from the same family could be so different. He worried about how much he was the same.

Target Equals Blank

The bus has nearly stopped in the slow traffic. The air conditioner isn't on. A rider opens a window. He sticks his head out and says, "You guys are doing an excellent job. You, yeah. You are doing great work. You are great people. Keep it up."

The man, in his forties, has never thought to brush his tongue.

Michele wants to see what he sees, to learn what he wants to encourage. She looks out the bus window, in the same direction the man in front of her is looking.

The bus crawls by a Pepsi truck that is pulled over to the curb for a delivery. Two men are unloading big pallets of pop. They turn to see who is calling. They hear what the rider is saying and are puzzled, cocking their heads then pulling their lips thin. They look at each other. One shakes his head. They go back to work. The bus passes them.

The man in the bus pulls his head back inside. He smiles to himself. He says, "Good job!"

FREQUENTLY ASKED QUESTIONS
(STRAIGHT GUYS)

- Are you a lesbian?
- Are you sure you are a lesbian?

- Do you get in trouble for wearing makeup?
- When did you know?
- Isn't it something that people can grow out of?
- Why are you so public about it?
- Are you going to have kids? How?
- Are you ever going to be really satisfied? You know what I mean?
- How many cats do you have?
- Did I already tell you that I am a lesbian trapped in a man's body?
- When did you decide to sleep with women?
- Are you trying to look like a man?
- If I hired you, would the fact that I am sexually attracted to you be a problem?
- Do you hate men?
- What do you think you might be missing out on?
- Why do homosexuals push their private lives on everyone else?
- Want to go out?

Michele is on her way to meet Ingrid. This will be their fourth time going out. Michele can feel a big crush coming on, but worries about conversation. Michele works with computer coding, and Ingrid is proud of being a Luddite, saying, "I wouldn't know where to find the on/off switch, and I don't care to look."

Michele gets lost in code, in its repetition and balance. In the fine ways it can be manipulated and the subtle ways mistakes are made and must be found then corrected. She likes it when the strings of symbols and letters that she types in disappear, becoming design when she puts it up online. How code unleashes all the dreamed-of colours and images and fonts and formats and links if she's typed and tested right. How it tells a story, even if it's a dull one. How it can build a strange thin structure with many rooms. She prefers to type everything out rather than use some program that does it for her. She likes to be the wizard behind the curtain.

Typesetters used to throw tiny letters upside-down and backward on trays, creating words, paragraphs, stories, pages, sections, and a whole newspaper or book or political pamphlet, just like that. But it was only when these trays of little letters and symbols contacted paper that meaning became clear for those on the outside.

Michele will kiss Ingrid's nose. She will message her scalp with the stubby fingers she has always been self-conscious of. She will say, "Come over to my place?" But first she will get off this bus and walk to the Malaysian restaurant they both like.

HTML is the major language of the Internet's World Wide Web. Web sites and web pages are written in HTML. With HTML and the world wide web, you have the ability to bring together text, pictures, sounds, and links . . . all in one place! HTML files are plain text files, so they can be composed and edited on any type of computer . . . Windows, Mac, UNIX, whatever.

From An Interactive Tutorial for Beginners
http://www.davesite.com/webstation/html/

```
<html>
<head><title>Target Equals Blank</title>
</head>
<body>
```
My mind is full of nothing. The men delivering Pepsi seem to do it the regular way. Maybe I'm missing something. Thoughts jumping around. No connection. Pop up, no weight.
```
<p>
```
I want to see Ingrid. I want this one to work. I'm getting old to feel like this.
```
<p>
```
Why do I think in code? Like dreams while learning French. Needing to pee but not being able to ask for a bathroom. Saying pregnant instead of full.
```
<p>
```
The code defines it all. Be positive. All in our own skins.
```
</body>
</html>
```

Ingrid has thick greying hair and bright eyes. She's in good shape because of her work. (She wouldn't be caught dead in a gym.) She is practical, and goes to protests. She has a gorgeous round belly. She has a fresh small scar near her right eye and a capped front tooth. She got the scar and lost her tooth at a protest against homelessness. A cop on a horse hit her with his baton.

She taped the TV news coverage the night it happened and played it back to friends for a couple of weeks. The video showed people pushing a barrier into an empty road, laughing. Then it cut to the mounted police charging through the whole crowd, swinging batons. That's when Ingrid would say, "There, see? The protesters are getting violent!"

Ingrid read in a paper the day after the protest that the situation had been "seriously deteriorating" when the police cracked down. She thought this was pretty funny. Like the situation hadn't seriously deteriorated enough to make the protest happen in the first place. Homelessness is one thing, but *pushing a metal barrier into an empty street*. Where will it end?

Ingrid is everything Michele wants, but Michele tries not to think this way. This will be their fourth date. Only their fourth date. She has a poster about the 1919 Winnipeg Riot hanging in her kitchen. Ingrid has lived here for only about a year. Before this, she spent major time in five different towns and cities, and she did a lot of travelling in between.

She never really wanted to settle down, but she got tired of shuffling her stuff around. She got tired of trying to prove she knows what she's doing with drywall, electrical work, and basic plumbing. When people ask what she does, she makes a point of telling them that she's a handyman. She loves to say it. She jokes that her company name is Hand Jobs.

Ingrid laughs when things fuck up. She drinks too much coffee. She keeps trying to quit. The stuff is hard on her stomach and makes her cramp more when she's bleeding. She's not sure which will go first, coffee or her period. She's not sure one will go at all.

Berberis vulgaris 6x is a caffeine withdrawal ingredient.

They met at a mutual friend's party. This is just their fourth date and it's been about a month. They are both busy people, so sometimes it's hard to figure out a time to meet. Hard to match schedules. They talk a lot on the phone. Now it's almost every day.

Ingrid is coming by bike. She left her tools at the latest site. She is watching traffic, but thinking about what happened today. She is doing some simple repairs for a straight couple. She's thinking about how she's going to tell Michele about the conversation that she had had before she left the couple's house.

It was a good one.

She thinks about Michele. Mmmm.

A car pulls close to the curb without signaling, then stops for a turn. Ingrid is cut off, so she knocks on the car window as she goes by on the driver's side. She makes a right turn later without sticking her left arm out in an ʟ. She realizes she forgot her helmet at the place where she's working, but knows there isn't enough time to go back.

Beer is like having a big bowl of cereal, except you get drunk.

Pears are like soft apples, but with a different flavour.

They both like red wine, and have gone through a half-litre carafe of the house. Their fingers have skittered across the back of each other's hands every so often during the night.

Then Ingrid says, "So this is what I've got to tell you."

"What?" Michele asks, a bit of worry in her voice.

"Oh, today, at work. You know, at this couple's house. I'm doing some bit-work there, odd jobs. They've got a bathtub and shower that's falling apart around the tiles. I'll be working on it in about a week."

"I hate when that happens," says Michele.

"Yeah, anyway, the guy can't say caulk. He says, 'cawhl-k,' like that."

"No!" Michele covers her mouth in this really sexy way. She's laughing with her head back, showing her neck.

"Yeah. He says, 'When you get to the cawhl-king, Ingrid,' and, 'Cawhl-king comes in a lot of shades, so I guess we should talk tone before you go ahead.' 'How did you learn to cawhl-k like that?'"

They are both laughing.

"So today, Jeannie, the woman, came home early and she was asking about the tub and shit. And out of nowhere I decide I need to deal with this thing and I said, 'Jeannie, could I talk with you about something?'"

"You didn't!"

"I did. 'Jeannie,' I said, 'you've got to get Hugo to stop with this cawhl-king.'"

"What did she say?"

"Well, at first she had no idea what I was talking about. I said, 'Please tell him that I do know the difference between caulk and cock. He can say the word right, you know. It won't upset me. I know which one goes where, and that's fine. No risk of confusion.'"

Each has an elbow on the table, arm rising, fingers laced one to the other's. They leaned into this position during the story and are laughing so hard, tears stream down their faces. They hold each other up.

They eat quickly. Get the bill, pay, and go. Ingrid walks her bike along. They are heading to Michele's place, without even talking it over first. Every so often, Michele squeezes Ingrid's waist.

They are too old for this. They are old enough.

Their story really starts once they get inside the door.

Technical Difficulty

When he sees this kind of shit, he just wants to hit somebody. But, like usual, Eric sits there, listening and shaking his head. Kathy's a talker. She talks back. "Ffff-ff-fff," she sort of laughs. Kathy does this by breathing out in short bursts with her top front teeth against her lower lip. Then she sticks her tongue out, points it to her upper lip, and leaves it there while she listens.

The woman on TV says, "Be imaginative. People have got to get out of the old work-ethic mind-set. Companies are not created to guarantee people work." She's wearing a smart but feminine business suit. She smiles a lot. She believes.

Then a politician comes on. He says, "The government can do only so much to retrain the workforce to get with the economy. We need real entrepreneurs. We need to be leading edge. It's getting tough out there. We need to fix the border. Investors are increasingly cautious." His eyebrows are tight together. His hair is thinning but tidy. His tailor-made jacket owns him. He talks about high taxes, the brain drain, tightening immigration to restore the market's confidence, and how workers aren't loyal to companies anymore.

"What I want to see is a survey." Kathy looks over to see if Eric's paying attention. He is. "I want there to be a survey of all these politicians, who all seem to agree about this shit. I want to know just how many of these assholes can really use a computer by themselves? How many of them actually did start their own business? How many know that most folks on this earth don't even have fucking electricity?"

"Hah," Eric says.

Kathy and Eric don't have a computer themselves, but their kids use PlayStation and the family goes to the library and goofs around with its system every once in a while. When Kathy and Eric go to the employment centre for jobs, they use a computer to go through the listings.

The news item ends. Now there's a discussion panel. "Here to take a closer look at the challenges we face in these extraordinary times is our regular panel," says the anchor. His head is tilted. He ends with a lopsided hint of a smile. Cut to another camera. He swerves his chair over to his right. Cut to a camera that pulls out and around him. The panel sits across the table from him. He introduces them, including the same woman who was in the news item. The camera closes in. She almost fills the shot.

Eric bites down on his lip. "I hate that bitch," he says.

"Well, how about the four guys, Eric? They okay in your books?"

"I get your point," he says, real flat.

The couple sits at either end of the couch and listens to the panel. Eric shakes his head once. Kathy breathes out a *ffff-ff-ff*. There's one guy representing unions, an economist, and some journalist who did some kind of investigation. The woman speaks for business. The anchor carries things along. They all seem to agree that the economy is in a dip, maybe a recession, and that some people aren't adjusting to new realities. The economist says that maybe the people out east should move if they really want work. He says, "It should be obvious that the region is done for. That's all there is to it. Government handouts for this kind of thing should be in the past. They drain needed resources from security and defence. You either believe in this country, and make it work, or you don't."

"What exactly is an economist?" says Kathy. "I mean, what do they actually do?"

Eric says, "Nothing that I've ever seen. Talk about how other people should do stuff, and how it's better if they don't get paid much for it. Unless they're the boss." Eric knows that Kathy's going somewhere with this. He likes knowing what's in her head. She's a sharp one, his friends always say.

"Shit," says Kathy. "A man doesn't need a regular paycheque to spout off opinions – any of us can do that. It's inefficient," she says. "I bet you that guy is paid by the government. I bet he gets a big cheque for sitting around having opinions. The new reality is that us unemployed-threatened-streamlined-downsized-cap-sized workers don't give a shit what he's thinking. Do the tax-payer a favour and give him the boot. See how he likes it, waiting in line and being grilled about how hard he's looked for work. Maybe he can get a high-paying, low-taxed job in the States. They deserve him. Blowhard."

"Hah," says Eric. "You should have a show, Kathy – *On the Dole, with Kathy.*"

"*Doling with the Doll*. No – *Doling for Dollars*," she says, "some kind of game show."

"Shh, shh, what's he saying?" Eric bends forward to show he really wants to hear, that he's serious. He moves his ear closer to the TV and kind of winces a little, like he's making an effort. It's because he heard the word consideration, and it came from the union guy. Not that Eric's all for unions, but he wants to hear what the guy says. At least it'll be something about workers being the same as other humans.

The economist interrupts the union guy. "When you say consideration, what you mean is more social spending, and the government just doesn't have money for that kind of thing. We are part of a global security effort right now and rightly so. This propping up people who won't work – that's the old Canada. And we're in an era of international trade under high risk, remember. Make no mistake about it. The stakes are very high."

"We've got to take the spending we already have and use it more creatively. Encourage small businesses. Lower taxes. Secure borders but make sure goods flow smoothly. Tighten immigration," says the woman. "It's time for a kind of tough love."

"Just wait one minute." It's the union guy. "What do you mean by that? How many coffee shops, craft stores, and failing e-businesses do we need in this country? This new economy you all crowed about a year or so ago turns out not to be all that, anyway. And it seems like this new Canada is spelled 'u,' 's,' and 'a.'"

The businesswoman says, "Who could have predicted what happened? Our friends and neighbours need our support right now. No need to take cheap political shots."

"Our neighbours need support, but our workers don't. Exactly my point."

She says, "How could you! At this terrible time!"

"Make no mistake about it, it's a complex issue," says the journalist. He has more to say.

The union guy keeps talking. "For all this talk about technology and information and knowledge-based whatever –"

The business representative cuts in. "Are you saying that using your intelligence is a bad thing? Are you saying that teaching people to do things for themselves is a bad thing?"

"What are you talking about? Is someone going to own a factory and run it all by their lonesome? We do still make things.

That's what's shipped across the blessed border."

Kathy gets up, fast. Her hands are balled into fists. She's squinting and her teeth show a little. She's mad. "I can't stand this anymore," she says. "Why doesn't he tell her to go to hell? She doesn't have a clue."

Eric pushes the mute button. "He – he doesn't have a clue either," he whispers, head down, rubbing his eyes slowly. "You don't really get a clue till it happens."

"I can't stand it anymore." She's not looking at Eric. Her eyes are on the TV, but she's not really looking there either. She's looking at what's behind it, behind the screen. The panel continues, miming its discussion. Kathy's quiet. Then she says, "I guess everybody thinks the TV is full of little people when they're kids. I did. Just like everybody. But the joke is, those people on TV are really the big ones, the big shots. The ones who count. Not us." She turns away, goes to the kitchen.

The host mouths, "convergence." Panel members throw their hands up and appear to laugh.

When Eric hears Kathy open the fridge, he decides it's okay to do some surfing. He can't stand to see this bunch yapping. He keeps the mute on. He just wants to check whether there's anything worth catching before he turns the set off. He clicks around. There's a battle scene from the movie *Kelly's Heroes*; one of the tabloid shows; some diet show; the religious channel with the banner "Pray for Enduring Freedom" and phone numbers scrolling at the bottom of the screen; a weird video; too much news; Osama bin Laden with a bull's-eye graphic on top of him. Before Eric knows it, fifteen minutes go by on mute.

"'Fifty-seven channels and nothing on,'" he says, still clicking.

"What?" Kathy says. She's got something in her mouth.

"Nothing," says Eric. "Springsteen."

151

"Oh, yeah. Right." She still has something in her mouth. "You want anything?"

"Nah. I'd give anything for the Juice Man though."

Kathy drinks something then says, "What's with you and that guy? That's that liquefy-everything-and-be-as-dull-as-dirt thing, isn't it?"

"I don't know. It's funny. I like how hepped he is about a blender. I like seeing the audience all enthused. I think about the kind of compost the pulp would make."

Kathy says, "That's on real late. I haven't seen it for a while. Who wants to live to be a hundred, anyway? Especially these days."

Her husband doesn't say that he's sure he sees an old girl-friend in the audience of the Juice Man's show, and that she's looking great.

Eric's in serious surfing mode. He's not looking to see what's on. He's looking to look. He wants to stop doing this kind of thing, but somehow reading a TV guide is slower, even though it usually ends up taking less time. But he doesn't see as much in that time. Something finally catches his eye. He's about to take the mute off when Kathy says something from the kitchen.

"What's that?" Her voice isn't loud; it's hissy. She doesn't want to wake up the kids, but this way Eric knows it's something important. When he gets up and goes to her, he finds out he's got a leg cramp.

"Shit," he says.

"No, listen," says Kathy. "Something's going on outside."

As he says, "I don't hear anything," Eric hears it. Like some-one creeping around. "Shit," he says.

"Well, let's go take a look."

They've had problems with animals getting under their porch

and at the wiring. Eric's limping because of his cramp, but Kathy doesn't notice.

Kathy and Eric stand at the back doorway. The night has a coolness to it – summer's almost over. They don't see anything, so they go out onto the patio. The houses in this neighbourhood are close together.

"Over there," says Eric.

"Shit," says Kathy, "it's them. What're they doing?"

Since moving in about a month ago, their neighbours have been a pain. The husband doesn't like to see Kathy do hard work. "Where's your husband?" he says. "That's a man's job."

Kathy once answered. "He's in the kitchen, cooking."

The neighbour stomped over to the front of the house and rang the bell. When Eric got to the door, wearing an apron smeared with tomato sauce, the guy said, "I don't like how your wife talks to me. You shouldn't let her."

Eric had no idea what the guy was on about. "You got a problem with Kathy, you talk to her," he said.

The neighbour looked disgusted. He turned to go, saying over his shoulder, "She wears pants." He said it just loud enough for Eric to hear. Eric shrugged his shoulders and closed the door.

Later that day, Kathy mentioned what happened in the yard. Eric told her what happened at the door. They almost pissed themselves laughing. Even so, they wished he didn't live beside them.

Things had only gotten worse since then. Tonight the guy is out with his wife and son. The daughter – their eldest child – must be inside. She has an early curfew. The three of them are not on their own property. They are in the yard next to it. That house is rented by two women the guy calls whores. They're away on a trip. Kathy and Eric are taking care of their cat; the couple knows the pet is outside.

The man and his teenaged son are wearing pajamas. The woman has a nightgown on. All three are in billowing white as they move around in their slippers. Only their hands and heads are uncovered. Her dark hair is tied back in a tight greying ponytail that the wind pulls at.

They are looking down.

"What could they be doing? It's not even their backyard," says Kathy.

"Hey, what are you doing?" asks Eric.

When the neighbours turn, Eric and Kathy notice they're all holding baseball bats. The woman's nightgown sometimes hides the one she holds when the wind hits it right and the cloth wraps around her arm.

"Hey, what are you doing?" Eric says again.

Kathy whispers, "Maybe it's the cat."

The two of them push further down their yard to get a closer look. At this angle, a streetlight shines through the narrow walkway between the other houses. Legs, arms, and torsos show through the neighbours' clothing. The couple sees that the small raccoon is cornered. It's been around the neighbourhood for a while, probably abandoned by its family because somehow it lost its tail. Kathy leaves food out, she feels so bad about how thin it is.

"Jesus, are you crazy?" says Eric. "What do you think you're doing?"

"We were just checking," says the man. "We heard some noises, and then we saw the animal. We came to see if it was okay." He looks panicky.

"Bullshit," says Kathy. She's thinking about how the boy had to straighten up before turning to see her. She's sure they're about to do something evil. "It's not your place. If you don't get out of there right now, I'm going to call the cops. If you try to do anything to that little raccoon, I'm going to call the cops."

The woman keeps looking down, with her arms by her sides. The wind still catches at her edges. The son looks over at his house, frowns, and starts clicking his fingernails. The man shifts his feet, looking like he's not sure what to do. He's upset – probably because Kathy is bossing him around in front of his family – but he can't look directly at her or Eric. Maybe he's also worried about what the police might do to him, this not being his property and all.

After a brief silence, the neighbours go home, dragging their bats behind them. The raccoon stays huddled in its place for a bit, then raises its nose and sniffs. It looks around and decides it's safe. When it runs, the raccoon crosses the neighbours' back-yard, then disappears across the road.

The Language of Safety

Three people on the forty-second floor are excited about their new jobs, but one is also afraid. She is worried about the curtains of glass that ring the building. On a windy day, the building gently sways. This day is calm. The new employees aren't.

A man in an expensive suit says he is Bob. He is orienting the three. He took courses in order to do this. He is proud of how good he is at giving new people a sense of the company, the office, and themselves. He can see that one woman is very jumpy. He senses that it's because of how high they are, and the glass, and the feeling she could fall. He's been through this so many times. He has a routine. He asks them all to step into his office. It is on the outer edge of the floor plan, snugged against glass. The jumpy one stares at the window. She tells herself to breathe right.

"We have a low-key but professional environment," Bob says. He is smiling at a private joke. "Style matters. So does confidence. We want our people to be confident. There's nothing to worry about here with us. Nothing." Bob suddenly runs full-force at the glass, from one end of his office to the other. He gathers speed. He twists his upper body around, throws his shoulder into the massive pane. Bob is looking at them. His eyes sparkle. He is saying, "See?" But Bob keeps going, through the tinted golden glass. He goes down. The last things that the nervous employee sees of

Bob are his eyebrows up, his mouth open. Not fear. Surprise.

The three new employees stand there stupid for seconds that seem like hours. Then she walks. Others are coming to Bob's office because of the crashing. But she goes to the receptionist and says, "I quit." The screams start. She makes sure to exit the building on the opposite side from Bob's office window, which is now on the ground with what's left of Bob. She hears the sirens, but doesn't see the point.

She takes time off. She stays home. The police come over and ask why she left that day. She tries to explain, but they tell her what she is saying doesn't make sense.

"A guy falling out a skyscraper window after he runs into it to impress people doesn't make sense," she says. "I wasn't thinking straight. Are you telling me that never happens to you?"

One of the officers admits, "Responses aren't necessarily always rational at all times." The two officers give her a business card, then leave.

Late one afternoon, she is listening to the radio. She hears a report about a subway train that just crashed. There are few details. There is a lot of smoke. Some people are trapped. Emergency crews are having a hard time doing their job. It is very hot in the tunnel: it's a steamy August day to begin with. The reporter thinks this might be the city's worst subway accident. Like it's a contest.

She wants to turn on the TV to see what's going on, but she also doesn't want to. She doesn't want to see blood or hear screams. She doesn't want to see stretchers. Instead, she imagines them when she tries to fall asleep. She is in the dark hot subway with something pierced through her. She is Frida Kahlo, underground and untalented.

She doesn't have a car. She doesn't have a love interest. She doesn't live or work in high buildings. She doesn't have many friends, and likes it that way. She chews her food and chews it. She is forty-seven. She gets hot flashes. Guys still whistle at her: she ignores them.

She has a job in a family's shop now. Only three steps to hop up and a glass door to pull when she starts her workday. She's okay with the glass at ground level. She brings her lunch so she only pushes against the door once a day. To get to and from the shop, she prefers surface routes. Sometimes in the winter, when it's very cold outside, she'll take the subway to keep warm. Otherwise it's strictly buses and streetcars, unless it's nice out and she has lots of time. Then she walks.

It is a bitter January day. She is tired and wants to get home. Her last customer sneered while she served someone else. Threw purchases on the counter and flicked a bank card her way. Stood with arms crossed, head tilted back. Pulled out a cell phone.

The employee ran the card through the machine. It didn't take. Ran it again. The customer stopped talking on the phone and said, "Is there a problem here?"

"I'm sorry, but your card isn't going through."

The customer hit the hold button on her phone and hissed, "But that's impossible. I have a ten thousand dollar overdraft."

"Well, it's not going through."

"Who needs this shit?"

As she was leaving, the customer carried only her purse and cell phone. She banged into a display case on the way, making a serious mess. She didn't apologize.

Now the employee locks the glass door. The wind cuts. She decides to go down. In the subway, the platform for northbound trains is crowded. One train arrives, going southbound, then another, then another. At this time of day, most people are going north. The people on her platform are edgy. They are too close to each other. They are angry every time more people arrive to wait. They look at the passing trains on the other side with hatred.

She notices mice running around the tracks. One is big, four others are little. The little ones are a lighter grey; the big mouse almost looks like a charcoal brick. Sometimes they run to each other, then run away. Sometimes they run right over each other. Cute.

The tracks pull at her, make her want to get down there, if only for a moment. She thinks about the power of the third rail. She wonders how it feels to lie between the tracks with a train coming.

Finally, a train crawls along, but doesn't lose momentum. People crowd closer to the edge of the platform, trying to get in the best position. Then they see the red destination sign: Not in Service. Bodies sag.

She kicks away some garbage that has swirled around her shoe. The real train comes. When she and the others get in, a man's elbow jabs her right breast, but she knows it isn't personal. A baby cries. Someone's coughing, and it sounds like it could catch. Try not to think about it. The train is too hot with everyone wearing heavy winter coats. She has to fight her way through to get out at her stop.

She knows that traffic is bad these days, but she's hoping to shake this trapped feeling, this feeling of helplessness. She's heard people talk about their cars. She's seen the commercials with the slogan, "Buy freedom for only $249.27* a month." She knows this is stupid logic, but it still appeals.

She talks to her sister on the phone. Her sister keeps going on about a new dog that loves to run. There aren't many places for the dog to be loose, so it goes along the railway tracks. This is a problem, because the animal doesn't always come when called and trains can appear, fast and sudden. They've had a couple of close calls. But the dog is happy.

She tells her sister that she's starting in-class driving lessons that night. Her sister says, "No. No, really?"

"Really," she says.

"Well finally, you're ready to admit you're an adult."

"I've always been an adult," she says. "Just one without a car. There's a few of us around, you know."

"Not by choice," her sister says. "The thing is, you choose not to drive. Very weird."

That night she learns that signs and lines are the language of safety. It sounds so easy. Diamond-shaped, octagon, rectangle; red sign, orange sign, green, and black; broken line, solid line, yellow line, and white. Watch the arrows, they show what to do. Watch for the line running through a sign, it shows what can't be done.

She belongs in this world.

She is in a doughnut shop, eating a low-fat banana-bran muffin and drinking coffee, even though it's dinner time. There aren't many people here. But she feels comfortable in places like this. She likes to read here.

The bell at the door jangles. It jangles again, then again. Four seated male customers and the girl behind the counter look up. A man is struggling to come in. It's difficult for him to get through the door because he is carrying a full-grown Canada Goose under his left arm. The goose is wriggling to get free.

The girl behind the counter shouts, "Get out! Get out!"

The man finally makes it through.

His eyes are big and he is dirty. He hasn't shaved for a few days. His left arm is tight around the goose. He raises his right hand, curled into a fist and says, "Fifty bucks, or the goose gets it."

The people in the doughnut shop stare at him. He says, "I mean it. Fifty bucks or the goose gets it!" He looks around. Blank reaction. "This goose will get it, I mean it," he says, then sloppily punches the goose in the head. "See?" The goose struggles harder, but it's trapped.

The reading customer who is afraid of heights says, "Don't do that. I'll give it to you."

The man with the goose says, "You better or –"

She says, "Don't do it again, or the deal is off." She stands up. "We'll have to go to the bank machine, though. I don't have the money on me."

She leaves her book behind.

They cross the street. The machine only gives out twenties. "Here's sixty," she says.

He takes the money with his right hand, shoves it in his pocket, and then hands her the goose. "Thanks," he says, then runs away.

The police are there in no time. Someone in the shop had called. The animal-welfare people come soon after that. They say the goose is apparently fine, but they'll take it in for overnight observation.

She takes a shower that night. She knows that birds are filthy and carry many parasites. She worries about what she breathed in when she was holding the kidnapped goose.

She doesn't watch TV or read the papers or listen to the radio. She has no computer, no cell phone, no Palm Pilot. She doesn't like gossip. Still, she hears about things: mad cow disease, E. coli, Hantavirus, Ebola, flesh-eating disease, West Nile virus, the return of TB, the mutations in AIDS, the rise of certain cancers, anthrax, smallpox. She keeps her house clean and tries not to touch anyone. She cuts back on red meat. She thinks about eating only organic foods. She thinks about not eating. She walks outside with a gloved hand covering her mouth. She drives her car as much as she can, hoping to avoid contamination.

Walking by newsstands a while ago, she saw photographs of large animals piled high, burning, and crying farmers holding newborn lambs. They were going to die anyway, she thought. Is it sad because they didn't reach human mouths?

She dreams of a man falling; buildings falling; everything falling. She dreams in a dark and grainy green with bright fuzzy yellow bursts. In sleep, her arms and face are covered in blackened blisters or running red sores.

She doesn't know where to go, where to hide.

Retired

The dust went under things, into corners, where light filtered through only on bright days. Rita began to leave the drapes pulled across the windows. Harder to see details. She put 40-watt bulbs in fixtures. She started to let the dust be.

The walls were once a sharp apple-white, the trim a chocolate brown. The chairs had been a mint green with little dark brick-red cushions. The big slim couch had been a cheerful pink with shiny grass-green cushions. The curtains were once soft marshmallow pink, with green, brown, and yellow accents, shot through with a fine red thread. Everything had blanded out over time. But the plush beige carpeting in the living room was still beige. The smoked mirrors behind the bar at the side were still smoky.

It was all smoky, because Rita smoked. And now it was all dusty, too. She didn't Pledge the coffee table, corner tables, kitchen chairs and table. She didn't wipe down her bedframe, vanity, or bureau. No Fantastic on the mirrors or windows in her flat. She hadn't even heard of a Swiffer. Sometimes it took her months to get bedding and towels into the wash. Rita didn't use her linens anymore. They were so stained and worn that she could almost see hairs sprout from their dark shadows. But she still kept them, just in case.

She had tried for most of her life to keep disorder at bay, but now Rita was retired. No one had really noticed her work before, and now nobody knew she had stopped. Her husband was dead.

She didn't know where her son was. He hadn't sent so much as a card in years. She didn't have anyone over.

Rita kept to herself. She was friendly enough. Some of the other tenants even knew her name. The regular cashiers and delivery men at her supermarket knew her, too. Once, in the winter, she accidentally locked herself out when everyone else in the building was gone. She went to the hardware store with no shoes on. A salesman came back with her to the flat and helped her get in. He joked about getting practice as a kid doing B&Es. Ever since, he made a point of waving if he saw her. This made Rita feel special.

Other than some small adventures, there wasn't much for Rita to do. She read, watched TV, went for walks to keep in shape. Sometimes she went to one church or another. She hadn't warmed up to lady ministers. Rita wished Catholic mass was still exclusively Latin, for that matter. She was saddened to see that the Anglican Church had updated from the St. James version. She believed in tradition.

An old friend Rita bumped into suggested golf to fill time, but she couldn't bear even the idea of the game. Rita would rather study the shape of her nails or look closely at her walls and ceilings to see how the spindly delicate tendrils being spun from dust and cobwebs were coming along. She enjoyed seeing them drift with air currents or her own gentle blowing. Much better than golf.

Things were becoming untidy. While she wasn't a messy cook or a sloppy eater, bits and pieces of food found their way onto the floor and countertop of her kitchen. Sauces spilled. Crackers broke when she dropped the box. She watched the changes in her former workplace with interest. Rita didn't consider cooking a part of her former work, because she knew she would die without eating, and she didn't want to go through her limited budget by eating out too much. Even so, she tried to stick with prepared foods or eat raw vegetables and fruits whenever possible. No more fancy chicken, and certainly no meatloaf.

This night, Rita sat at the table eating a light supper of macaroni and cheese with tuna and catsup. It was later than she usually liked to eat, but she had been reading a good detective novel and had lost track of the time. She now held the book to the right-hand side of the pot she ate from.

Something caught the corner of her eye. She quickly raised her head, but there was nothing. She went back to the book.

Again, movement. This time, she was pretty sure she saw a little bit of something disappear into her stove's front-left element. She sat very still for a while, but nothing happened. Rita got up and walked over to the stove, listening for noise. She didn't hear a thing. She sat back down to her dinner.

The third time Rita thought something might be moving around, she didn't hurry to look. She kept her head at the same angle and slowly moved her eyes. She saw five little grey mice running around on the stovetop. She let out a sound, not a scream exactly. She wasn't scared. Well, she was scared, but not of the mice themselves. Their being *here*, on her stove, in her flat. Them in front of her.

One started to clean, curling up in a ball and licking down its tail. Rita let go of her fork. The sound against the pot made the mice run one behind the other into an element, but they soon came out again.

She grabbed hold of the fork and dropped it again. The mice did a little jump, then skittered away, but not as far as they had the last time. Rita dropped the fork again. This time, the mice didn't seem to notice.

Rita picked up the fork and slowly loaded it with macaroni. She brought the food to her mouth. She took it into her mouth, chewed, and swallowed. She did it all while looking at the mice. She finished her meal, leaving the detective book open on its spine, pages fanning, her place lost.

The little animals went about their business. It was as though she wasn't even there, until she got up to clear things away. The chair screeled across the floor and the mice took cover. Rita heard them tumbling as they went behind the wall. She did her dishes. She was retired, but still sensible. She wasn't going to waste her money on paper plates and throw-away plastic cups.

As she moved through her familiar kitchen, her ears and eyes were alert for any sign of the mice coming back. But it wasn't going to happen tonight. She went to bed, and dreamt of running in dark spaces.

The next morning was bright through the curtains. Rita almost didn't feel her varicose veins and arthritis. She dressed in a rose-coloured sweater set and burgundy pants. She put on her dainty dark-brown Hush Puppies. She decided to take a fast walk through the hilly old town of Orchard Mines, then give herself a treat of coffee, orange juice, and a low-fat blueberry bran muffin at the Tim Horton's on the highway. She put her hair up, smiling at her reflection in the mirror.

She was at the coffee shop's counter when she heard from behind, "Well, as I live and breathe, Rita Willis!" It was Reggie, she knew right away. Didn't even have to turn around, but she did, slowly.

"Reginald. And how are you this fine day?"

"Rita, I'm up to my old tricks. Can't complain, but that doesn't stop me. This and that."

"Good to hear," she said.

"What brings you out? Must be something grand."

"A walk, Reggie. It would be a shame not to enjoy what God gives us."

"Well, God must have given you something big-time to get you into Tim Horton's. You win the lottery?"

"No. I do not play games of chance. Just a little adventure, old friend."

Reggie asked her to sit with him. Rita accepted. Despite herself, she enjoyed it. Salty dog Reggie Phipps. She imagined what her dear departed would have thought, and enjoyed herself all the more for it. When she looked at her watch, she saw that two hours had passed.

"Oh, will you look at that!" she said. "I must be off now. I'll be seeing you though, I'm sure."

Reginald smiled. "You can bet on that, Rita. Even if you don't play the cards, you can bet on it. I haven't seen you this lively since you were seventeen."

Rita blushed. "We won't talk of that now, will we?"

"Ever the lady, Rita!"

She rushed home, still feeling the blood in her cheeks. On the way, she picked up some fresh vegetables for a salad and a bouquet of flowers.

The girl at the cash asked what the occasion was.

"There needn't be one," Rita said. "A woman can cheer herself up, can't she? Last I heard, there was no law against it."

"No offence, Mrs Willis."

"None taken, dear."

Back home, Rita had her salad and finished her book. She took a nap. Getting up at dusk, she saw mice in the kitchen again. This time, six of them.

"My, look at you," she said. She leaned against the doorway

with no door, crossing her arms and ankles. The mice chased each other around. They poked into everything they came across. They climbed the brick wall that spanned one side of the room, popping in and out of several holes in the mortar.

Two hours passed. Rita's stomach growled. She grabbed prepared baby carrots from the fridge, along with some luncheon meat. "Time for another mystery, enough of this," she said, then went to bed.

Life went along much like this during the next month or so. The number of mice grew. One day, she pulled back her bed sheets to find a stash of food. "Oh, you dickens," she said, but she was more annoyed than amused.

She found herself using a broom and cleaning cloth to deal with the droppings and the smell. She began to find shredded tissues and dust-mop fluff pushed into drawer corners and shoes. But while she was losing part of her retirement keeping up, she also felt she gained with the joy they provided. It seemed like a fairer exchange than the one she'd had with a husband and child. With this arrangement, nobody pushed a dinner away and said, "It stinks." Nobody yelled at her.

Reginald called. Before Rita knew what she was saying, she had asked him if he wanted to drop by Saturday afternoon. He accepted. She wanted to take the invitation back right away, but didn't, for fear of seeming foolish.

She went through the building, telling her fellow renters she would like to have a visitor on the porch in the coming days. She even asked one fellow if she could borrow his lovely outdoor teak chairs and table. Without exception, the people she spoke to were surprised and pleased that she came by.

Rita planned simple finger foods. She bought supplies, being sure to keep things in the fridge, where the mice couldn't find them. She dreamed of how Reginald was when she was young.

3:55 PM Saturday. The guest was expected at any moment. The hostess had everything set up on the porch and was bringing the food down. She put the platter on the table, straightened up, smoothed her skirt, then saw Reginald coming toward her.

"Rita!" he said. "No need to go to such trouble."

"No trouble," she said. "It's a pleasure when you know a person will enjoy it."

"My taste buds aren't what they used to be, but thanks."

"I'm sure you'll do fine. Better than some I can think of," she said.

Reggie said, "Everything got messed with when I stopped smoking twenty some-odd years ago. Nothing tastes right, and I use far too much salt for my blood pressure." He laughed. "Do you think as the big-man boy that I was back in our day, that I ever imagined I'd be talking such nonsense?"

"I don't recall you putting your mind to it, no." Rita smiled. "But you've always been on the salty side."

They had celery chopped up in one-inch lengths, stuffed with Cheez Whiz. They had peanut butter with slices of banana on saltines. For a sweet, they had maraschino cherries, pieces of canned pineapple, and tangerines wedges in raspberry Jell-O.

"Always such a cook," Reginald said.

"It faded away, I'm afraid, Reggie. It lost its charm. The last while —"

"Oh don't go into the weepy past now, woman. The charm is back! Something to celebrate! The chicken's laying eggs again, so we needn't worry about making her into soup yet, not tonight, anyway. Turn the boiling pot off, old girl."

"There are some things I don't mind remembering, Reggie." She looked at her fingers as she said this.

"I get your drift. You were always a saucy girl, in your sneaky way."

"Please, Reginald."

"Sorry, sorry." He paused, then said, "Rita, I hate to ask, but I'm getting kind of dry after such a feast. D'you have anything to drink?" Reginald coughed a bit.

Drink. She had forgotten all about it. She had bought neither pop nor proper coffee. She didn't have any milk in the fridge. She was in the habit of drinking water from the tap, without even a glass, just cupping her hands and slurping it down. So be it if the water killed her.

"I believe there's beer, Reggie. Is that still your drink?" Rita said this calmly, but she felt pure panic. If there was such an animal, it was left over from her husband's reign. He had passed on three years before.

"Perfect," he said.

"I'll just be a moment, then."

"Would you like me to help?"

"No, no, you stay right here."

On her way to her flat, a neighbour walked down the hallway with a laundry basket full of dirty clothes. The neighbour asked, "How goes it?"

Rita said, "Oh," with a shrug. "Who's to know?"

"Ah, the dating life," said the neighbour.

"Well, wish me luck, then."

"Hey, by the way, have you noticed any mice in your place?"

Rita shook her head.

They said their goodbyes. Rita rushed into her place and began the search for a bottle of beer. Deep under the sink, far behind the bottles of bleach and tins of silver and brass polish, she found two full beers in a six-pack of empties.

"Oh, thank you, Jesus," she said. She pulled one out and dusted it off.

Back on the porch she said, "I fear it's a bit warm, Reg."

The first pull was a big one, against the thirst. He coughed again. He took a few more polite sips, but Rita knew it was just for show. He didn't say what was wrong. She didn't ask.

"Better be off there, old girl. Harold needs me to drive him for a shop."

"Harold?"

"Dewson. His eyes aren't so good and he's got the diabetes. I help him with his errands. Duty calls. I guess that should be 'Dewson calls.'"

"You can kid all you like, Mr Phipps, but that is a very kind thing. Now you don't be a stranger."

"You count on it. Thanks for the grub, Rita."

Once he'd left, she brought the platter back inside with everything on it. She put it on the kitchen counter, and saw that the beer bottle was still three-quarters full. She remembered that she used to rinse her hair in beer every once in a while and decided to try it again. She washed the dishes.

Two days later, she found a dead baby mouse in a cut-crystal punch bowl she'd received as a wedding gift. It broke her heart to think of the little thing trying to run up the sides. She thought about how long it must have taken for death to come. She thought about what she was doing, how selfish she was, while this little creature suffered. She bleached the bowl.

The next day as a pick-me-up, she decided to try the beer out. She had left it open on the countertop, because she remembered it was better when it was flat and warm. She didn't want the shock of cold beer on her scalp. But the beer didn't come out smoothly for some reason, and without thinking she shook the bottle. Out came a baby mouse, glancing off her left ear.

Rita had been leaning over the edge of the tub. She almost fell in. She screamed and started to cry. She saw the little mouse, curled up as though it had fallen asleep, except its eyes were open and white. She screamed again, grabbed at the mouse, threw it into the toilet bowl beside her, and flushed. She turned on the hot water. Pulled down the detachable showerhead. Got into the tub, fully clothed. She brought the hot water to her ear and kept it there as long as she could stand it.

She shouted, "I can't take it."

She cleaned herself up. She dried her hair. She got dressed. She went to the hardware. She asked for some help. She got the poison. She came back home. She put the poison down everywhere, and waited.

Over the next few days, fewer mice came to visit each day. She watched their antics with love and regret. She saw that they were not getting into as much mischief, that they were losing their pep. Then, one day, there wasn't a mouse to be seen.

She thought of their corpses, dried out behind her walls, in her ceiling, under her floor. She did a big clean of the surfaces she could get to. She opened the curtains and shook the throw rugs. Rita rented a steam cleaner for her living room furniture and wall-to-wall carpeting.

She got up her nerve and called Reginald.

Lilly in Memory

peas
corn
patty
applesauce

She leaves a burner on high. It scars the bottom of the best pot and ruins the handle. Lilly's neighbour comes over when the smoke detector goes off. Lilly wonders why the stove is on, why the pot is empty. She isn't hungry. She doesn't have much of an appetite these days. No one makes her do things she doesn't want to do.

She is sleepy, feeling vague.

Lilly is watching Lawrence Welk. Everything is bright. Smiles sparkle but are not sharp. The singers are young and wholesome. Even when they dance, innocence shines through. There is love, but not that bad kind of love.

She used to watch with her John. Every night, reminded of times they never had.

During the break for fundraising tonight, she gets up. Who knows how long before things close in? Enough of Mr Welk. Lists to do.

GLAMOURAMA HAIR STYLIST

wash
rinse
set
Fridays, 11 AM

Her appointment is with Stephanie, who knows the colour is Ice Blue. Lilly forgets names sometimes. Lately, more and more. Of the hair colour. Of the stylist. She has been going for seven years. The address is written down.

MY NEIGHBOUR IS MARY

Mary will say, "Good morning."

I answer, "Good morning."

Mary will say, "And how are you today, Mrs Elder?"

I will answer, "Fine, and you?"

Then Mary will say, "Oh, fine, fine. I can't really complain." She will ask about the weather.

I must keep it simple. I will say the weather has been as expected. I will say I'm feeling it a bit. Then I will ask Mary about her husband.

Her husband's name is. . . .

Her husband's name is. . . .

Her husband.

He is not written down, but he is at home. Lilly hears him laugh and yell sometimes. Lilly hears him clear his throat and whistle. Lilly cries.

1981
PAID FOR
JE DECEASED
FUNERAL

Funeral Service	740.00
Casket	1035.00
Concrete Vault	245.00
	2020.00
Globe & Mail	29.94
London Free Press	11.30
	2061.24
Less Discount	51.75
	2009.49
Evergreen Cemetery	
2 graves	450.00
1 Interment	125.00
4 Cornerstones	50.00
	2634.49
Creative Memorial	
Headstone	
on ac	200.00
Paid Bal	459.00
Paid	3293.49

JE DECEASED
RECEIVED

Mutual Ins. Co.	3034.21
North Am. Life	3023.05
Church	
Group Ins	1010.25
Estate Death	
Benefits	1439.10

RECEIVED
1981

On the bottom of this page in Lilly's small black binder: "John died 6 June 1981." Long ago, she had been a bookkeeper in an Irish linen factory. More recently, she was the wife of a retired minister. Now she is alone. "Half of me is gone," she says.

The secret is, it's more than that.

She is a ghost fingering a photograph, crying. The tears fall onto the pictures, which are covered in plastic.

Lilly is looking at a house. She used to know it. She was born there. It had a name. She rode her bike from work. The geese chased behind her, hissing. She was terrified. But she can't remember them anymore. She got engaged. She waited nine years. Then John Elder came from Canada and took her away from there. She never returned for a visit.

She shook this place off, only to find it inside. But she is slipping. She is. It had a name. She was.

Colours then. Only colours. Everything, colours with unclear sound. A smile. It's somebody. Holding hands.

Dreamy

Johanna is at the controls of a helicopter without blades. A teardrop, sideways. I snap feet, ankles, and lower legs to my knees into the braces at the top of it. I have never done this before. Johanna lifts off, then goes forward slow, so that the wind isn't too bad. My arms reach out. I form a "t."

It's just after lunch and the sun is still high. It's warmer than it should be this time of year – the kind of day kids hope for on Hallowe'en. Within minutes, we fly over the tree tops of suburbia. We are high enough that I can see light jump against the waves on the lake. The island isn't far from shore, and it's possible to see fragments of some cottages over there through the trees.

Johanna takes us above a straight road. It's an older development of about forty years, and the trees lining the street have matured quickly, growing high above the regular roofs. Most of the houses are ranch-style brown brick set back deep within the yards. The driveways are dull broad asphalt sealed black against the weather. Each one ends with a quirky mailbox, painted to really stand out. It is well into fall and the leaves are grounded, past their reds and yellows.

Up here, the intricate weave of tree branches and the shades of bark and the crowns of the trees are beautiful in a way not seen from below. Because of the time of year, nothing gets in the way.

Something is coming up the street, something going down. On either side of the road, big figures, and then small ones beside them once I really look. The larger figures are stooped over. They swagger when they walk. Their necks almost don't exist. Their arms dangle to the ground and sometimes seem to anchor them. Their heads are strangely sloped. They are very interested in the trees. They are huge monkeys with regular-sized humans by their sides.

It looks like the monkeys are very orderly, going and coming just like they're supposed to. But then I see some start to reach up to the larger branches of the trees, lazily pulling themselves off the ground, even swinging. Some of the trees start to sway with the weight, looking like they could break at any time. Other monkeys notice the opposite line, are curious and can smell desire. A few cross the road, greet, and groom. The humans follow, pleading for reason but powerless.

Johanna and I pass over the monkeys, go beyond the suburbs. We are heading to a round tent near the lake. She flies higher, then banks. I see water and then sky. It feels like my legs have broken from the braces on the helicopter and I am floating alone. It feels like my body is flattening out and going up to the heavens, but not to a physical place. I agree with the Pope on that one.

But then Johanna finishes her manoeuvre. I have never feared when she's been in control. Even though we can't talk through this ride, we are connected. She is what a boy could never be for me. She is a girl.

We head back to the ground, where the tent itself is crawling closer and growing large. It was made for a circus, and has a red-orange triangle flag at its peak. The tent is hot pink. We land in a dreamy way, and it takes a moment before I realize it's time to jump down, then I do. Johanna gets out. We laugh about what we saw. The two of us walk to the entrance flap, where we are met by the assistant, who says, "He's ready for you."

Inside I am surprised to see that the tent has several sections, all a pleasant green-grey. The assistant fixes drinks, and we go into the screening room. The three of us chit chat. We are enjoying ourselves very much.

Stanley Kubrick arrives just before the lights dim for the movie. We say our hellos, then turn to the opening sequence of a musical comedy he's been working on. It features Sarah Jessica Parker, Julie Newmar, Frances Farmer, and other famous stars whose names I can't remember. The film is funny, reminding me of the Marx Brothers more than anything else.

When the lights come back on, we talk about the weather, the monkeys, the tent. I am thinking about how this film is a real break from the other work Stanley Kubrick has done in his lifetime. Then that makes sense, now that he's dead. The assistant prepares a fresh round of drinks. We talk about colour, patterns, and silence. We talk about men and women, and how it really doesn't matter. But it is everything.

Monk

I need a glass of water
I am a stranger to New York
the other day this guy talked to me sweet
and my skin seems kind of dry.

The first morning a cardinal woke me
the second evening dogs kept me up
Days are soured by saws, pneumatic drills,
a woman excited by a woodpecker in the park.

She was nice, that woman,
strangely chatty like Americans can be
There he is, she said. *There he is.*
Her head was tilted, her back bent.

The stay has been a pleasure
I don't know what I'm doing here.

It's raining –
there are sounds of thunder
but too regular,
coming from inside –
there's a ping ping ping on the air conditioner
I hear it's muggy in the heat.

By myself in a friend's apartment
in New York City with days to go
I choose a couch that could be nowhere
dare to write the word "alone."
This needs revision, and I revise it
one sharp Toronto day
mostly thanks to you.

Acknowledgments

SUPPORT | ENCOURAGEMENT | INDULGENCE
Ruth Castledine, Margaret Christakos, Lynn Coady, Mark Connery, Ian Cooper, Bev Daurio, Nadia Halim, Ruth, Alex, Beth, and Catherine MacDonald, Ward McBurney, Hazelle Palmer, Emily Pohl-Weary, Renee Rodin, Carole Sacripanti, Ann Stone, Helen Tsiriotakis, members of the United Jewish People's Order, Alana Wilcox, Zab.

INSPIRATION
Adults, animals, art, Aurora Ontario, Nelson Ball, Marc Bell, Jane Bowles, Brampton Ontario, Alex Bystram, Barbara Caruso, Chicago Illinois, Mark Connery, Dino, dreams, Edmonton Alberta, Lilly Elder, family, Moira Farr, friends, Lisa Germano, Michael Glassbourg, Betty Goodwin, Macy Gray, Dan Hall, P.J. Harvey, Patricia Highsmith, Graham Hollings, Eli Howard, Ruth Howard, Luis Jacob, Stanley Kubrick, Ang Lee, life and observations, The Loony Spoons, A.J. MacDonald, Lucy and Roberto Martinez, Suzanne Molina, music, Camp Naivelt, nature, New Mexico, New York New York, Manuella Oliviera, Outkast, Paris Ontario, the Penny Arcade, Liz Phillips, plants, Dan Quayle, Radiohead, relentless socialization in a chronically exploitative culture, Johanna Shapira, Colin and Laura Sims, St. Pascal Quebec, Toronto Ontario, Vancouver British Columbia, The Verve, Darren Wershler-Henry, what I've read, Windsor Ontario, work, the world, the Writers' Trust of Canada and, last, the Canadian Club.

PROFESSIONAL COLLUSION
For our beautiful creative marriage, thanks to the sunny Arsenal Pulp boys: Blaine, Brian, and Robert. Thanks also to the people of Ontario, who supported this book through the province's Writers' Reserve program. A toast to movie-man Jerry Ciccoritti. I owe much to the rabble at *rabble.ca*, who returned hope to my working life, and gave me time to write and stories to tell. Barbara Zatyko of *Geist* magazine cracked *Grey* open, even if she doesn't know it. Disinterested readers Kam Rao and Barb Linds provided sober advice and telling detail. Artists Lisa Smolkin, Amy Lockhart, and Graham Hollings gave the words their sister images.

Many thanks to all.

Credits

"Cockroach"
• appeared in *The Writing Space Journal* – volume 8/2, fall 2001 totem and ritual issue

"First Day"
• originally appeared in *Crash: A Litzine*, October 1997

"Flat Earth"
• originally written for *Geist* magazine, Number 35

"Monk"
• dedicated to Mark and Johanna
• an earlier version appeared in *The Writing Space Journal* – volume 8/1, spring 2001 homework issue

"Nursing the Wound"
• appeared in a self-published chapbook called *Work and Other Stories*, Three Rs Art, 1994

"Red"
• appeared as a poem in *The Writing Space Journal* – volume 8/1, spring 2001 homework issue

"Rolling Blue Concrete"
• published in *Canadian Forum*, April 2000
• made into a self-published chapbook called *Total Rejects & Rolling Blue Concrete*, as a collaborative effort with artist Lisa Smolkin, Three Rs Art, 2000
• illustrations and story from the chapbook were excerpted in *broken pencil*, Number 15

"Technical Difficulty"
• appeared in the self-published chapbook *Work and Other Stories*

"Terrazzo"
• appeared in the self-published chapbook *Work and Other Stories*
• ran in *Rampike*, Volume 9 #2, 1997

"There Is No Year Zero"
• written for the anthology *Carnal Nation: Brave New Sex Fictions*, published by Arsenal Pulp Press, Fall 2000

"Work"
• appeared in the self-published chapbook *Work and Other Stories*

About the Author

Judy MacDonald is editor in chief of *rabble.ca*. Her first book, *Jane*, a novel (Arsenal Pulp Press/Mercury Press), was nominated for a Rogers Writers' Trust Fiction Prize and will someday be a motion picture. She graduated from Edmonton Kindergartens Ltd. on May 28, 1970. In grade two, she "contributed that extra 'spark' every class needs." She was a "considerate and co-operative young lady" in grade three.

photo by Graham Hollings taken at the Penny Arcade